TO WHERE WE ONCE BELONGED

TO WHERE WE ONCE BELONGED

COLWYN BAY REVISITED

CINDY LOWE

Matador
9 Priory Business Park
Wistow Road
Kibworth
Leicester LE8 0RX, UK
Tel: (+44) 116 279 2299
Email: books@troubador.co.uk
Web: www.troubador.co.uk/matador

ISBN 978 1784623 883

British Library Cataloguing in Publication Data.
A catalogue record for this book is available from the British Library.

Printed and bound by CPI Group (UK) Ltd, Croydon, CR0 4YY
Typeset in 11pt Adobe Casion Pro by Troubador Publishing Ltd, Leicester, UK

Matador is an imprint of Troubador Publishing Ltd

*To my parents. Bob and Mary, with love and gratitude
for bringing me up in Colwyn Bay.*

'Time, which changes people, does not alter the image we have retained of them.'

Marcel Proust

FOREWORD

This novel is inspired by certain true events which happened in my home town during the Second World War, some of the characters are based on people who lived, but the names have been changed, others are purely fictitious. For example Alf's story of the information bureau is based on information given by the late Albert Rigby (who was very enthusiastic about promoting the story), but all of the Gerard family are a fiction.

In chapter 4, Beryl's conversation while making cakes with her grandson is a memoir which inspired all my research on the Ministry of Food and the vital function of the town. It is a fact realised only in recent years that the town of Colwyn Bay and its population deserved huge recognition for its vitally important role during wartime in feeding the nation. Of the many who relocated here and later left to return home in any decade, or those who were lucky enough to grow up here, all have great affection for the town.

This has become more apparent to me from my association with the Heritage Group in Colwyn Bay, and also the many messages and contacts I received after my book *Colwyn Bay Accredited* was published in 2010. There was such a great response and wonderful stories came from so many people who were so enthusiastic in telling about those days, and still more are being told! Many situations of the mixing of the population and changes in division of labour reflected situations of social change all over the country.

Some of our contemporaries who were not born during the war said they would love to know more about those days, so here is created a fiction based on the truths told, which compares aspects of the present and how the town is now, with how it was then. Of course great changes happen everywhere and continue to do so, but let's go further and imagine a future. I hope we will be around in 2039 to see the celebrations of the centenary of the Second World War and the results of ultimate changes for our town.

Although some may consider change has not always been amelioration, the old and the young have great affection for this small, low profile but wonderful town, if they care as much as they seem to then would they please get involved in any way they can for its continuous improvement. If anyone has memorabilia similar to that of Muriel, which they think no one would value, please give it refuge with the Heritage Group.

The poem in chapter 20 was written by the late June Lee and published within this novel with permission of her son Roger, to whom I am grateful for helping me with copy editing. The diary entries from the First World War, particularly poignant, in Chapter 5 are genuine, from a great uncle, Percy Grisenthwaite of Coldstream Guards.

Thinking of her roots Rita gives us a starting point with her fond memories and her wish to be reunited with her family. Back in the nineteenth century nostalgia was thought to be a mental illness, an idea to which we do not subscribe today. Southampton University has carried out a long term study about reminiscence work which proves beyond doubt that people are heartened by reminiscing.

Stories about your own locale certainly increase pride and community feeling greatly, but imagine, there could be people living on your street who have their story ready to tell! Just ask them, but please be sure to record it and share it. We look forward to it.

Cindy Lowe

Colwyn Bay

Carefully opening the lid of her trunk and releasing the leather bound item from its acid-free tissue paper she felt a shiver go through her, and Alexis pulled her robe closer around her in her boarding school room in an effort to ward off the cold, but it was not the temperature that had the chilling effect on her, it was the excitement of what she was about to read. She had hardly noticed being cold as she, Alexis turned the page. She was thrilled to be reading her great grandmother's diary written during the years of the Second World War. In these modern times she must have been an unusual girl, although youthful she had a special and passionate interest in this subject inherited from her grandmother that wise and nurturing woman who had had trustingly handed over to her not only this precious volume, revered among her family for its importance, but it gifted her with that inherent seed of a burning curiosity, of a craving to gain valuable insight of how things once were then for others of previous generations during those very difficult years, and especially as it was written by her own great grandmother. She could never actually understand why some people would not want to know of the past, why couldn't they have her fascination? She so wanted to share her enthusiasm. Alexis had not inherited her physical appearance from her grandmother, but instead had the dark Irish good looks of her grandfather's family, also local to this small town on the North coast of Wales, but she certainly had her grandmother's temperament. As she read on her glittering green eyes scanning the material and relating it to the little knowledge she had already gained she became engrossed, yearning to know more. She knew only what had been told to her over the years. Why, oh why hadn't she listened more closely? She reproached herself, and she vowed to be more careful in future, and to ask her grandmother pertinent questions about the characters she had seen described here, yes she would have to make notes, after all Grandma Faye would not always be there to ask, and she dreaded that day. It was no good asking her Dad, he had never been interested, but she was grateful to him for sending her to the boarding school in Colwyn Bay, the town of her grandparent's birth, while her parents travelled the world with Dad's music career. Living here at boarding school had created a bond between the grand daughter and grandmother while Alexis' parents worked abroad. Returning her attention to this leather bound diary embossed with the date was unlocked a first-hand account written by another young girl who had no idea what the years would bring, but written from her own unique perspective, and Alexis tried desperately to read between the lines and to gain an insight into attitudes and psyche of the writer and her family during those days. The writer had at the time no idea of the seriousness of the situation, or of the possible outcome. Looking to the future had brought her no answers, but even now, looking to the past there would always be some aspects, some secrets that would never be known.

Alexis herself wondered what had gone on there and then in the Bay, and more about her family during the war years, reading this was one way to find out just a small fraction of it. Yet it was just the view of a wartime schoolgirl, now read by a present day fourth generation descendant student. She speculated, at the time she would have been almost the same age as the writer of this diary. Everyone has their story, their particular viewpoint. Looking back, some who had experienced those times may disagree about what really happened, did their memories play tricks on them or was it as crystal clear as the day after it happened?

The people here in Colwyn Bay had had a flurry of activity in trying to communicate with the future when two schoolgirls in 2010 had had an idea of what to leave as a legacy. Alexis knew there had been information set down in the year around the time of her birth a Time Capsule was speculated to contain certain items, not yet to be opened for many years. Her grandmother had told her what had been enclosed; being privy to secret information due to her heritage role, but what would those items tell anyone? Timetables, tickets, menus and receipts? Regeneration plans? Now those would be interesting to compare to the actual progress made. But what about attitudes to events happening at the time? Alexis would have to scout the editorials of the local papers as her grandmother had done for her own research into wartime. The time capsule was stored at the local theatre. What could it tell us? How many of us will be there to see it opened? Many families and especially those who have not moved on to other addresses for a number of years have precious artefacts in their loft which are at risk of being lost, abandoned, destroyed, ...unappreciated. But those who move home often and quickly are not so circumspect having more urgent and pressing issues in their minds, and they may unknowingly discard valuable items.

Puzzling now over descriptions of the town, it had as had many areas (any judgement on civic management aside) changed almost beyond recognition largely due to social *ideals*.

More than a few of the important buildings remained, and here they were mentioned at intervals. If walls could talk, and if some of them had not already been demolished, and if only diaries could tell to us messages from *between the lines*, above and beyond what their writers had first intended. Had the writers been worried about being judged on their comments in the future? Would we? Once written they were open to interpretation rightly or wrongly.

As for the town itself, these days some wanted it to change even more and to wipe away and obliterate its very distinctive character, those were the people who never looked up beyond the shop window fronts, never took any interest in the fantastic architecture, only thought of the finances of everything and value of nothing, as in the famous quote by Oscar Wilde. Some even had no idea of the important role the town had fulfilled, which had been almost secret at the time. Had the townspeople, and the others evacuated to carry out the important war work not risen at the time to the challenge then the future would have been grim indeed.

Frowning she puzzled over the squiggly shorthand inscription, Pitman's style. Even Grandma Faye wouldn't be able to decipher this although she had learned back in the 1970s but her knowledge had atrophied. What secrets did these lines hold? It was something to do with her great- grandmother's girlhood friend. Would this and other mysteries ever be revealed?

Alexis scooped the wing of raven-dark hair behind her ear and frowned at the difficult-to-decipher neat but inky handwriting. Pausing she glanced out of the window, it was dusk and people were switching on their lights in the early Spring evening. An apartment building across the road converted from a large house had several windows lit up already. Alexis with her vivid imaginings encouraged by her grandmother began to speculate on the story behind each of the windows, and not just as a present day happening, but each had a rich and varied history behind it, some ignored, some deliberately hidden. How much of their own family did each of the occupants know, they would know little of the previous inhabitants of the building? After all everyone's lives really were extraordinary.

Alexis reluctantly rewrapped and stowed the diary carefully away under lock and key. It was precious, and she returned diligently to her homework. *History of World War One and World War Two*. Thankfully local areas were being recognised for their particular input. Local people here had had a part in this and it had inspired Alexis. She now knew what she wanted to study in the future.

CHAPTER 1

Costa Blanca back in 2009

Margarita placed the Spanish lace bookmark on the page then closed the book with a snap and lay her head gently against her velvet wing back chair, her white silky hair in stunning contrast to the jewel-rich velvet colours. She glanced around her study arrayed with antiques, awards and objects d'art collected on her extensive travels, and with her career in entertainment. Her eyes were tired from reading, she considered the novel on her lap, and it wasn't that sensational, not in comparison to her own life. Then, dwelling on a line of poetry from her youth which now had resonance for her.' She would 'take down that book and read'… It was warm and humid in the room the heat drained her, she certainly felt her age on this day. She put down her novel and instead she allowed herself to 'read' into stories from her own past, to reminisce a little about her life as she so often did these days, travelling in her mind in wonder at the journey she had so far enjoyed with its seismic ups and downs. She found it easier these days to remember events from long ago, even from her childhood than she did to recall what had happened that very morning. Reminiscing, about places she had enjoyed in her childhood, and the daffodils worn on the first of March she remembered another meaningful line of poetry, describing it just as she experienced, her thoughts flashing upon her inward eye. Solitude, there was much of that these days, which gave rise to a good deal of reminiscing. It was certainly a less exhausting exercise than dashing around. She had done more than her fair share of travelling in her life and she was almost eighty now, and had been a widow for some years. She could not get around adventurously like she used to, not that she couldn't afford to do it in some luxury. She had the means but not the energy or enthusiasm. She had enjoyed a successful career and had also made a good marriage, so she was more than comfortably off. In truth she didn't actually know her net worth, and never thought about it, didn't monitor it as she had people to do that for her. Maybe she should. She looked down on her hand at the gold wedding band and accompanying engagement ring with several large sparkling diamonds in a row, thinking about her late husband in the days she first met him when neither of them had a bean, but they were so happy, then she rose from her chair and approached an antique chest of drawers made of highly polished wood. Opening the second drawer she picked up a notebook and flicked through the words of the many songs she had known in her life, stopping at one in particular, which appropriately described her thoughts and feelings about her souvenirs. She reflected that her life seemed full of possessions and memories, but somehow was now strangely empty.

There was a particular song from the late 1950s which also used to be in her own repertoire which described the poignancy of her present situation. At the time it was written she hardly understood those lyrics, describing the way mementos vividly brought to life her past, her youth. Here were the letters tied in bundles with blue ribbons, a pressed flower in tissue paper with the petals drained of colour and memories both poignant and vivid rose up to confront her. '*What was left now?*' she thought.

She had to make a plan, some decisions for change. She was a determined woman, whatever action she chose, she would make it happen. She would get Faye her carer, (or her P.A. as she liked to think of her, since she certainly still dealt with a lot of correspondence from fans even now) to arrange a small gathering for her birthday. This would be a start. They would have room to stay over for a few days in the guest suite, airline tickets would have to be arranged, provided they accepted the invitations of course. There were friends she did not see very often these days, with whom she had not met since her husband's funeral, and as for family – she had lost touch with her only remaining brother after an argument which got out of hand. What a fiasco that had been, she put it out of her mind for the time being, but would come back to thinking how she was going to deal with it later.

She waited for friends who could make the journey to come to her now, although many of them were of a similar age. So there were not many visitors. She lived quietly, not as she had in her hectic past. Always there had been concerts, engagements, performing and recording, being managed constantly. But she had loved her career as a singer while it lasted. As a small child it was something she had never dreamed would happen to her. There had not been the opportunities those days, not where she came from, an area of Liverpool near the docks, and in the days long before Merseyside was 'on the map' for popular music. There was no *X Factor* then, no such thing as '*Britain's got talent*' nor '*Pop idol*' no she even predated '*Opportunity knocks*'. She had had quite a large following, a fan base. It was in the 1950s that her career had really taken off and especially in the 1960s when her hometown Liverpool had been well and truly put on the map. When in her early twenties she had produced first record albums and then in later years' CDs, she had even had film parts in America. She had been lucky, and all because of the war when her life had changed dramatically.

Margarita had been born in 1930 in one of the poorer areas of Liverpool near the docks. She had become involved in entertainment at an early age, during wartime, and quite by chance, during the evacuation. She could not have been housed with a better family; none could have been more caring or supportive than that where she and her brothers had been taken in. The older daughter of the family had taken Margarita under her wing and encouraged her as a diversion from the war and from the separation from her mother. It was to be an amusement for them both. They discovered to everyone's surprise, her own included, that she had a superlative talent, of which she might never have known if she hadn't been escaping the bombing in Liverpool. Mary, her teenage mentor at the same time discovered her own aptitude for teaching and after a dancing career went on eventually to have her own ballet school later in life. Margarita had first of all copied the older girl with dance steps, like a little shadow, and then was allowed to accompany her to the concerts to watch, while she performed. Many had been held by the Ministry families at the 'Castle Hotel', and on the Pier and also in the local theatre in Colwyn Bay. There she had heard singing, which had inspired her, and she discovered to everyone's amazement that she herself had a beautiful voice. The civil servants had in the few years they stayed energised the area and brought a great deal of culture as well as employment opportunities. All the middle class families did not want to discontinue what they had started in the south in the 1930s whether choral singing, amateur dramatics or orchestras. Yes, thought Margarita, they certainly were good days then. Although she hadn't been at all sure when she had first arrived on that station platform in 1939 as an evacuee with her two young brothers.

On that day in 1939 as the steam train pulled away from the platform of Colwyn Bay station a crowd of excited children milled around, shabbily dressed, and carrying small cases and bags. Cries were heard *'Where's the sea?' 'I've never seen it before, show me, eh is tharr it? What's over the other side?'* Each one had a bulky brown box slung with string diagonally over his or her shoulder. The sound of the train leaving the station to return to Lime Street echoed a shrill note and a black column of coal fuelled smoke rose in a billowing spiral. On the station platform, a lone child stood, miserable and confused. The sound of excited chattering Merseyside children faded away as the others all marched to the hall where they were to be allocated to local families, so that the weeping of a little girl gradually became audible, and it was evident that something had upset her.

Emlyn Jones's heart melted, a local family man a loving father of daughters walked over to the child and in a kindly voice tried to reassure her, which was an overwhelming task. She had been uprooted from her family and everything she knew, and was taking it worse than any of the others. *'There there, whatever's the matter? Don't cry now. Perhaps you can come home with me. Dry your tears on this handkerchief. I've got a girl at home, how old are you? Would you be about seven?'* The child, wearing a roughly stitched nametag which read *'Rita Gerard,'* looked affronted at this suggested estimate of her age, stopped crying immediately and glared at him while she considered it and then retorted hotly, *'I'm nine, and I want to go back to Liverpool.'* She then immediately started crying again, even louder this time as she felt she had even more reason now, and it seemed she had a very good pair of lungs, and a strong spirit. She was insulted; someone had thought her to be two years younger than her real age. Her shining copper coloured curls shook and trembled on her velveteen collar on the coat which seemed obviously too big for her, a hand me down.

Emlyn Jones tried then to reason with her. *'Why's that then? You don't want to go home; you will be safe here with us'.* Rita was not so sure about this, and she thought she had very good reason, and stopped her crying again to say *'Isn't this Jairmany?* Her voice lilting upward.

Emlyn was amused at her misconception and pronunciation but tried not to let her see he was laughing inwardly, the poor child was upset enough already and knew that being mocked would not help her. *'Why do you think you have been sent to Germany? Germany is a very long way from here; no one will send you there.'* So Rita told him of her suspicions. *'Well, people are speaking in this funny language, like ... foreign.'*

Although it was true that there had been some foreigners in the town, Rita would not yet have had the chance to encounter them. Emlyn Jones quickly realised what she had heard, it would be some of the local WVS women who were discussing arrangements for the evacuees had been having a conversation on the edge of the platform. ' Beth yw'r broblem? Beth sy'n bod?' asked the tall lady in grey. She seemed agitated.' Yr wyf yn edrych am rai pobl fynd â nhw' the other had said. Emlyn heard them, realised that the billeting officials were struggling with their overwhelming task and told Rita, *'Don't worry, this is Wales, and they are speaking Welsh. We are not far away from Liverpool, just across the water, see there, just across the platform over there is the sea and then Liverpool beyond.'* He shouldn't ask her this, not before the billeting people for the WVS had approved, but he knew that his family would have to take an evacuee, to do their bit, and he thought this girl would be a friend for his daughters, so against his better judgement he rashly offered *'Will you come home with me to my wife and daughters?'* He looked around him realising it wasn't an option she could easily refuse since there were few people left at the station, they had all gone down to the pier pavilion where billets were being allocated, yet his empathy told him he would not like to see his daughters having to go through this experience, being foisted off onto complete strangers. He was immediately thankful that he had been born and bred in this part of the world, that his family had not had to relocate, and in gratitude for this did his outmost to help those at risk. But Rita had conditions for accepting his generous offer and told him in no uncertain terms. *'No I can't. Well... yes, ... only if I can bring me two brothers, me Mam says I have to look after 'em.'* Rita had taken very seriously her responsibility and promise to her mother that she would look after them and she then shouted loudly to two younger boys, her brothers who were scuffling, unperturbed by their predicament. She caught the younger one by the collar; he couldn't have been more than five. The older one, about six years old had put on his gas mask and was blowing rude noises through the rubber. He well knew it wasn't a toy. All the children had been told they may need them to protect them from a gas attack, which had featured so heavily in the fighting of World War One. Fortunately, but unbeknown to them those masks would never be used in the 1940s. *'Here, our Billy and Jimmy, come here, stop scratching, and don't fight, we're to go home with this nice man. It's alright he's not Jairman. This is Wales.Pick up your gas masks and put them away.' 'If it's Wales then are there fierce dragons here then mister?'* asked the older boy.

Emlyn Jones was shocked. If he took these three lively scallies he would have a house full, how would they cope in his small cottage. *'Oh, Oh wait a minute, er... I don't know if I can take you all, er... I am not sure,'* he was embarrassed ' *...you see we only have a small house, I really don't know where I will put you all.'*

Rita, mortified, started to cry again, more loudly this time, she was beginning to come round to the idea of living in with the family of this kindly man, and now he was withdrawing the offer. It was all too much for her. Luckily Gwen Morgan, a WVS supervisor approached the scene in the nick of time with a clipboard in her hand looking very officious. *'Oh here you are Mr Jones, yes I have you down on my list as agreeing to take some children...will you please take these three with you? We should go down to the pier pavilion to make it official, but these three lagged behind. Everyone else seems to be there now, they have picked out their children, and I know I will not have enough placements. They sent far more this time than we expected, far more than we can accommodate. They said five hundred today, but thirteen hundred arrived overall on the three trains, so the billeting arrangement has not run as smoothly as we would have wished. Where they are going to be put I just don't know.'* Emlyn capitulated, he didn't know what else to do, and his Welsh heart had thought a minute ago with empathy, 'What if it were his children standing on some strange railway platform somewhere, and all the people who had said goodbye didn't know when they would see their loved ones again'. *'I don't know what Jenny, my wife will say about this. Well, I suppose we have to do our bit. All right, we will help. Come on children we will go for the bus. Billy! Jimmy, stop fighting! let's go to the promenade and get the coach. And I'll show you the pier.'*

* * *

The revival of those old memories always caused a poignant sadness to arise in Margarita. The younger brother, Billy, had been taken back to Liverpool quite early on in the war, as had so many children. His mother had come for him, he was only five and he had missed her and she him. She was expecting another

8

baby by then. That was the last time Margarita – or Rita as she was known as a child – and Jimmy had seen their mother. In May 1941 between the first and the eighth there had been extensive bombing and Rita's family had disappeared, feared dead. Rita was fourteen by the time the war ended, and with the help of the local people she applied to stage school and was accepted with a scholarship. Her family circumstances had generated a certain amount of sympathy for the young Rita and Jimmy. Jimmy had done well too with encouragement; he had been younger, only twelve at the end of the war, but his continued education had led to him applying to university, which would have been unheard of in his previous circumstances. The extended family in Liverpool had been supportive of them both after their home was bombed. Their mother and little Billy were presumed dead after a raid, and their father ... well ... they hardly knew him. He had never returned from the war.

After university the other brother, Jimmy had married a student he had met there, a lovely girl called Susan and their daughter was born when they were in their twenties. By then he had qualified as an architect. She was thrilled that they had called their baby Maggie, after Marguerite and they had a close relationship, especially as she had no children of her own. Maggie grew up and married at twenty-five, and soon had three children of her own- two girls and a boy. Her youngest, a son was called Liam. Yes, Margarita recalled, he was called after her brother Billy, or William, because they all remembered that Jimmy always used to talk about his lost brother when Maggie was a child, particularly when they were on holiday. He would start with the story of 'Peter Pan' then somehow the conversation always came round to his own 'lost boy'. Jimmy had taken the loss much harder than even Rita, as the two little brothers had been very close when they were young during the start of the war. Margarita remembered how she had cried when she thought she might be separated from them at the North Wales station, and then Emlyn Jones had taken pity and taken them all in. How different her life would have been without the influence Emlyn's daughter Mary had had on her. She wondered what happened to the family, she had tried to keep in touch, but apparently Mary had married a man who had worked with the Ministry, one of the locals, and he had been transferred to Guildford after the war then she lost touch with the Jones family.

Sadly now history had seemed to repeat itself with the separation. Although she hadn't been in touch with Jimmy in recent years since she had been living abroad, and also because they had had 'that' argument. Unbeknown to Margarita Liam had disappeared some time ago, and Maggie's family were beside themselves. They had tried the missing persons register but to no avail, and he was not on Facebook. Apparently Liam didn't want to be found although many attempts had been made by his nearest and dearest.

Jimmy's daughter had blamed herself and said Liam never should have been named after his great uncle, then he wouldn't have 'disappeared' too, but there was more to it than that. Liam had not fared well as a youngster. Although he had had a good upbringing, and exactly the same as that of his two sisters, who were happy and settled (one had become a pharmacist and the other a dental nurse), he was always in trouble and the police had been involved sometimes. He hadn't done well at school, even with the encouragement of his parents, never had a decent job and couldn't provide for himself. His mother used to say to him 'don't think the world owes you a living' and 'you only get out of this life what you put into it', but to no avail. Both Maggie and her husband had studied diligently for their careers, and had also worked at holiday jobs to contribute to their student life, although Jimmy and Susan could have supported them they believed in kids learning a '*work ethic*'. Susan had eventually in desperation facetiously said of her grandson – '*Oh, Liam, he wants to be a brain surgeon*', when acquaintances asked what career he was going to follow, because it was an embarrassment that Liam could not settle and would not accept jobs which were within his sphere. Then sadly he had gravitated even lower; he had got mixed up in the drug culture. How different she thought was Liam from his parents and his grandfather Jimmy, who had been brought up with few advantages and lived in poverty but thrived on education when he was given a chance. Maggie had had a phone call from one of Liam's school friends who was also searching for him, hadn't found him on any of the social networking sites and during the conversation had mentioned that Liam had spent time in Wales. This is exactly where Jimmy suspected that most likely he would be. Jimmy had always regaled all his grandchildren with stories of the war and the evacuation when they had been about the same age as he had been when he had moved there, because he had a huge affection for the town. In subsequent decades there had been a drift of young people from Merseyside to the North Wales area where there were plenty of unoccupied houses. Large boarding houses were no longer needed for the tourist trade now that everyone was going to Spain, Florida or elsewhere, to other more exotic destinations, so the accommodation became houses of multiple occupation where landlords were happy to rent to individuals on benefit. The town like so many others on the coasts of the UK had experienced a downward spiral. But because of Liam's previous track record this arrangement with its company of similar peers would suit him to a T. No wonder Jimmy suspected Liam might be there.

Margarita was not to know the outcome of the row which had caused Liam to leave home. She hadn't intended to dwell on the misfortune of Jimmy's family, but felt for her brother in the troubles with his grandson, even though she had no children or grandchildren of her own. But nevertheless she felt his family were also hers, didn't they carry the same genes for goodness sake? and she empathised with their anxieties, she felt to the ultimate extreme that was possible for her in her own experience. There was bad feeling there now which she regretted bitterly. She shifted in her chair uneasily and got up slowly, stiffly, shouldn't sit too long these days, she must keep moving, she thought in her agitation and regret. She went back over to the drawer and opened it, again looking among her treasured possessions. Not those with monetary worth, but the most important, things of sentimental value. Letters from her late husband, in bundles tied with silk ribbons, and small mementoes of her early life. While she dreamed of the soft look their eyes once had, the bars of the song returned to her memory and translated from his native Flemish she remembered the words '*Some precious keepsakes will always be within my treasure chest, and though they try to give me consolation, I cry, and tears fall on a broken heart. I find both sadness and joy among my precious souvenirs.*'

Here through the tears that fell she spied a box containing a shiny ten euro silver coin, one of the many gifts her husband had given her on their wedding anniversary while they were staying in Belgium, and she remembered that it commemorated sixty years of peace, depicting the Phoenix as a representation of a new Europe, post 1945. As she remembered the mythical bird has, in many cultures, long been represented as a symbol of rebirth, immortality, and renewal. The reverse of the coin showed a map of Europe. "*Belgium*" in the three official languages was displayed as well as the value of ten euros, surrounded by the stars of the European Union. This immortal bird whose rare appearances signify peace and prosperity never becomes old or dies. It is said that its rebirth out of ash, symbolizes the constant striving spirit. Thus inspired she retrieved the velvet pouch and box where the coin should have been kept, reunited the two and put them safely away. While the seed of an idea germinated in her mind, she shuffled towards the kitchen to fetch refreshment and poured freshly squeezed orange juice from a jug in the fridge adding ice cubes from the dispenser on the front of it.

Still pondering on the bird, which is central to myths and legends in many countries and cultures, she was reminded that her husband had regarded it as a symbol of the world being rebuilt after the Second World War. Margarita set her IPod on to its docking station and the classical music resounded, it seemed appropriate to the moment, then taking her glass across the room she leant and looked out through the French doors over a balustrade on the semi-circular patio, which surrounded her villa. The lights of the nearest town twinkled on the distant shoreline and it reminded her of decades ago when she had looked over the coast towards Liverpool from Colwyn Bay, not knowing what was happening to her mother and younger brother. Here in Spain the weather was getting even hotter. It was a relief to avoid the cold British winters and she had a choice of destinations where she could do so, it was pleasant to live here in the Winter and Spring, but now in June the Costa Blanca heat exhausted her, and she did not relish the thought of how overwhelmingly hot it would be in Spain soon.

Later that evening Rita awoke with a shudder, she had been dreaming, no it was not a dream but a nightmare! She felt panic. There had been a shadowy figure stalking her, not a monster but a pretty young woman, in her late twenties, with long dark hair. She didn't know what this woman wanted, or whether she could give it to her and she wasn't threatening, just mysterious. She didn't recognise her as either of her nieces, Jimmy's daughters, who took after their mother's side of the family, but strangely Rita felt that this person was something to do with Faye. Now she knew Faye had only one son, no daughters. Rita lay awake for a long time after this dream, perplexed and trying to interpret it and to work out what was it the woman wanted, and also what she herself wanted. Eventually she achieved a decision, it came to her, as inspiration often does in the small hours when the anxious are restless, and sleepless. She wanted to be reunited with her family before it was too late. The argument, the family feud, had already gone far enough. She decided there and then she wanted to take a trip to Britain, to Liverpool. She would dearly love to get in touch with her brother and his family, reconciliation was long overdue, and maybe she would also go to Wales. Travelling in her mind was no longer enough for her, she had been in reality everywhere in the world she had ever wanted to go. Reviving her constantly striving spirit she wanted to travel back in time to revisit her roots to go to where she had once belonged. She wondered, but could not imagine, what was going on there now.

CHAPTER 2

It would take a miracle

Colwyn Bay North Wales. 2009

Saturday 8am

A helicopter whirled loudly above the village circling repeatedly. It crossed the park, but did not make for the coast or open sea. It hovered above the buildings. Uncharacteristically, this was no air sea rescue, which the locals had become accustomed to seeing take place once in a while. The weather was mild; it was early in the day. Few boats were at sea, but no one needed rescuing – well not from the sea anyway. An elderly man, Alf, was awoken suddenly by the noise, with a jump. He had come here to visit for some relaxation, but had dreamed he was back in the war years and that a German bomber, a Heinkell III was overhead jettisoning bombs on its return from a raid on Liverpool, the trauma had stayed with him into later life. When fully awake he finally realised where he was and that it was 2009, and relieved to be safe, relaxed luxuriating down under the covers, thankful that he didn't have to get up for work, he would have another half an hour sleep and then go down to the sea, for a walk, to get the paper before breakfast, as he did every day.

Thursday 10.30am

The holiday season should have started by now and Alf

wondered if it would ever get underway. It wasn't busy although there was so much talk of the British holidaying at home in these days of the credit crunch, '*Staycation*' was what they were calling it. Alf would have liked a deckchair, but there were too few tourists around to warrant an attendant this early in the season. He would have sat by the sea and reminisced. He was unwilling and too old to be without the comfort of a chair. Cut off from the beach these days; the divorce of the town from the shore had been absolute since the expressway had been built in the eighties, cutting a swathe through the area with no further access roads allowed by the planning permission. He maintained his view that sometimes it is better to travel in one's mind than in reality, and revisiting nostalgic sites can sometimes bring bitter disappointment. It was certainly not as he remembered it.

Unrecognisable since Alf's day, with only a footpath and no road for vehicular access leading down to the promenade, there were barely any signs visible in order to direct strangers to the seashore. Only the locals knew the way for certain. It was as if the beach was kept secret, because on it there was an obvious and embarrassing eyesore like the proverbial '*elephant in the room*'. Immediately opposite the railway bridge was the old derelict pier. Alf had lived away from his hometown for many a year, and recently planned to retire here with his wife. He had many emotional ties, which vividly sprang alive when he returned. He had brought up his family in the south after a being transferred with his government employment, but in spite of the changes he encountered he still found his way to the beach and walked over to the shingle near the pier. At least there were still the vast expanses of golden sand to be seen when the tide was out, and he would look forward to that. He sat down wearily on a bench and opened the paper, which was published weekly on a Thursday. He had not seen this local rag recently since he and his family had lived in the south for so long and he had seldom returned to this small seaside town on the North coast of Wales. *'Petrol station hit again by knife raiders'* – he read and deduced *'so that's what the helicopter was looking for on last Saturday morning.'* He had heard it circling overhead above the quiet retirement community of neat semis and bungalows with manicured colourful gardens. He went on reading, sadly shaking his head. There was no pride in living in this town these days and he wondered why people couldn't appreciate this potential paradise they lived in and what brought about their sad situations and noted further *'Vandalism, violence, addiction related crime, drugs, fraudulent benefit claims,'* wondering what drove people to this, before he turned as an alternative to the obituaries. There he noticed the demise of a good many elderly people, one or two over a hundred years old, none of whose names he recognised. So, in celebration of this longevity he concluded that it may be a healthy place to live out one's retirement, until one's nineties and beyond, with the cleanest of sea air; but viewing his surroundings it was beyond his belief that his good memories could be shattered in this way.

He had been brought up here before the war, when his family had relocated from Lancashire in the 1920s. In those days Colwyn Bay was a salubrious area. He and his family had been proud and glad to live there. Yes, he had a good many fond memories of the place but the rose tinted view he had carried with him was evaporating rapidly. He looked over at the pier pavilion, one of the few left in the country, but sadly dilapidated, in fact downright dangerous. He calculated that in a *'lose lose'* situation it would be costly to demolish it, but also to renovate it. The northern towns were lagging way behind the south in the regeneration stakes, but perhaps it would happen. It would take a miracle.

Alf then by association allowed sweet reminiscences to flow over him like a blossom-scented breeze. He had met his beautiful wife during wartime as had so many of his contemporaries in this and in areas all over the country. Alf found her here, the love of his life, in the pier ballroom at a dance during the war. They had been very young when they hurriedly married during his brief period of leave from the navy. They had been lucky enough to celebrate their 65th wedding anniversary. He wondered how many other marriages had started out that way and felt so fortunate that his had survived so many obstacles – the war, and separation, reduced economic circumstances, and a quality of life transfer with his work to a completely new area. As a reminder of the romance which had mesmerised him melodies of Glen Miller played like a loop in his head, but he was dragged down to earth with a bump as they were eclipsed by the reality of contemporary music which brought another reminder of when he himself was young here on this promenade, where he had had his first kiss in a promenade shelter and he looked back at the way his life had unfolded.

The music encroached from a young man's Ipod nearby. Although the lyrics had some resonance for him he still thought *'Why didn't he put his earphones on?'* he was, slightly irritated by the loud music. Jet skis zoomed with a modern buzz across the expanse of sea. The incoming tide was approaching fast, so a walk on the sand was out of the question for a few hours at least and in this grey and chilly weather it was not tempting. Plump, dazzlingly white and grey seagulls cried their raucous warning, while circling and signalling imminent rain. It would have been nice to have some company, thought Alf, perhaps he should go and get a cup of tea before the rain shower started. He wandered over to the kiosk and sat at a steel table. A few feet away was another younger chap, in a sweater and jeans, reading the same local paper and shaking his head despondently. The two men looked at each other, over the top of their newspapers, both equally craving company and possibly having something in common.

Alf took a chance and said *'It's very pleasant here, I like to relax and enjoy the scenery. I am getting on a bit – nearly 90,'* he exaggerated, *'and past tearing around.'* The other chap nodded in agreement and said, *'Aye, I know what yer mean.'* Alf detected a Merseyside accent as their conversation progressed and encouraged by any kind of response went on *'What about you, you must be about 20 years younger than me?'* This was a generous estimate, the chap nodded again and to get his age in perspective said, *'Yes but I like to take things easy now that I am retired.'* Alf went on persistently trying to encourage conversation with the stranger. *'I used to live in Colwyn Bay and have a great affection for the place,'* after a pause. *'That's why this is a nostalgic visit trying to remember what happened many years ago; and so much did happen especially in the war years. We do like to talk about the war! As a young boy where did you spend your schooldays?'*

The other man at last looked a bit more interested in pursuing the subject now and said, *'Funny, I am here for the very same reason as you,'* he lied. *'It's not far to come from Liverpool, I live on the Wirral now. I have been back here often enough, but this time I thought I would look up old haunts.'* He didn't want to disclose his real reason for coming here to anyone; it could wait until later, if he were to continue the conversation... or he might just keep it quiet. They got into conversation:

'But the town was seriously disrupted; it was never the same again really. I clearly remember the day war broke out... are you old enough to remember that?' ... *'Well I was a very young kid at the time.'*

Alf remembered it well. The appeasement policy of the

1930s had failed and by late 1938 Hitler was planning the annexing of the Czechoslovakian Sudetenland, which had been taken from Germany after the Great War. Chamberlain had flown to Germany to sign the Munich agreement with Hitler, relinquishing control of Sudetenland to Nazi Germany. It was signed at 1.30am on 30th September 1938. Chamberlain asked Hitler to sign a peace treaty between the United Kingdom and Germany. He agreed. Upon his return to Britain, Chamberlain delivered his famous 'Peace for our time' speech to delighted crowds in London. After Czechoslovakia was invaded in 1939 Britain had warned Germany against further attacks and when six months later Poland was invaded the British and French governments declared war. Alf's family had listened fearfully to Chamberlain's famous broadcast at 11.15am on the morning of September 3rd 1939.

"I am speaking to you from the Cabinet Room at 10 Downing Street. This morning the British Ambassador in Berlin handed the German Government a final note stating that, unless we heard from them by eleven o'clock that they were prepared at once to withdraw their troops from Poland, a state of war would exist between us. I have to tell you now that no such undertaking has been received and that consequently this country is at war with Germany. Now may God bless you all. May He defend the right. It is the evil things that we shall be fighting against, brute force, bad faith, injustice, oppression and persecution and against them I am certain that the right will prevail."

* * *

On that Sunday, many were in church for the eleven o'clock morning service all over the country. In the local church of St Paul some of the regular churchgoers thought there was additional reason to pray, others were shocked and had not predicted what had just happened. As usual that morning the bells had tolled before the service, and before the broadcast, calling in the congregation who had duly arrived. The church was especially well attended, many feeling the need for prayer. The day was crisp and bright and the hymns were as usual sung in good voice. The opening hymn for that morning had such gentle calm words but the peace of mind was about to be shattered.

'*Please be seated,*' said the vicar as the hymn came to an end. '*Before we go on with our service I have some dreadful news. It's my unfortunate duty to let you know that while this service has been taking place, our Prime Minister Mr Chamberlain has broadcast on the radio to the nation. We are now at war with Germany. We do not know what this will mean for each one of us, it is too soon. From what I remember from the last war we will need all the courage and support we can get from each other. Your church will be there for you at all times and you know that I shall be here for you whenever you need me.*

'*So let us pray silently for a few moments.... Let us pray for all service personnel ... for all our brave sons, husbands, brothers, friends. Amen. Now hurry home to be with your loved ones – they will be waiting anxiously for you.*'

A woman was hysterically sobbing at the back of the pews. People could not help but talk in hushed tones even before the vicar had finished what he was saying. Shock rippled through the building, although many had half expected and dreaded this news, others were numb with disbelief.

Olwen Owen turned to her friend next to her and in disbelief said in her softly spoken Welsh accent; '*Well now who would have thought it would come to this?*' And in response her friend Jenny Jones replied, spoke her thoughts and her hopes.

'It really is still a shock although we were half expecting it,' then optimistically, 'in my view it will not last that long. Six months at the most. It might be over by Christmas.' Their husbands had been sitting together and at the end of the service left to walk deep in their own conversation discussing their own plan of action. The wives walked sedately behind them. Olwen and Jenny left the church with the others in stunned silence speaking to the vicar on the way out and they held out their white lace gloved hands to him in the porch. Jenny said to him in honeyed tones, 'Thank you vicar, that was a very comforting service. I am sure Mrs Bowen thought so too.' (Mrs Bowen, a widow since the Great War, was the woman who had been crying.) The gravel crunched as the two women walked down the pathway between the graves, Jenny was silently thinking of loved ones who had been lost in the great war and Olwen said to her, 'Whatever's the matter with her, Edie Bowen, we all could see this coming.' Jenny answered her quietly since they were still within earshot of others. 'Well, Ed Bowen, her son went over to Belgium last week on holiday with his wife. He is a teacher you know.'

Olwen was incredulous: 'Oh why did they do that at a time like this? Do you think it is possible that they will be able to get back here, safely?'

And Jenny could only answer, 'Who knows? What about those lads who joined the Territorials last year? They'll be in the front line in no time poor devils. But what about the French, I heard they have built some defences, they call it the Maginot line, to prevent the invasion of Alsace and Lorraine; we'll soon know.'

Olwen went on, unable to leave the subject of Ed: 'Didn't Ed Bowen know there was going to be a war on? We all expected it in our house, he should be here now, the school term is starting soon.' Jenny patiently and quietly responded, 'Well some believed Chamberlain *when he came back with that piece of paper. But no, be prepared. My older daughter wants to enlist in the ATS now but her father doesn't want her to go away, and she can't go without his permission'*

Olwen now continued in a different mode, as one who was young enough to have no adult recollection of the first world war, and said frivolously, *'The youngsters are excited to leave this quiet place. Nothing ever happens here in Colwyn Bay – until this. But we will all be expected to work now.'*

They walked further down the road towards the village, now out of earshot of the other churchgoers. Walking quickly, they wanted to be home to discuss the radio broadcast with their families. They also had to see to the Sunday lunch, which would be expected, and in Olwen's case by her boarders. Olwen thought about all the chores she did with help from her daughter. She had been up since six that morning. *'We **do** work don't we? It's just that we don't get paid for it.'*

Jenny had to agree. *'Yes you are **so** right there. But I mean we will have to go **out** to work, proper jobs, you know.'* The war would change women's lives more than they could imagine, and permanently. Thinking of all the unpaid chores she had yet to complete that day, Olwen was beginning to get irritated with her friend now. *'What are you talking about Jenny, we work all summer, and we have our boarding house. My husband says we will **all** be expected to take in evacuees from Liverpool. All that area is going to be a target for bombs with the port and all the shipbuilding going on in Lancashire. Or they may come from somewhere else, there are a lot of families looking for somewhere to live, they are from Manchester, and London too.'*

Jenny had something further to add to this. *'Yes, All the relatives from all over are turning up on people's doorsteps. Out of the blue, surprising us all after not seeing some of them for years, not even a phone call nor a Christmas card, yet there they are with their baggage on your doorstep.'* Jenny had some experience of this as she herself had English relatives.

Olwen thought for a minute before saying, *'And who can blame them? And if they come... well they are family aren't they? We have to take them in.'*

Jenny was excitable and apprehensive, understandably after hearing the news and dreading what the future would bring. She and all the other women of the town would do what they could. *'Of course, but the town will get full up. Can we cater for everyone? We better get home quick I need to see to my linen cupboard.'* *'And check your blackouts too,'* called Olwen after her. *'We have some of that luminous paint left, I can let you have some for the doorbell and the clock'*

CHAPTER 3

Memories of the information bureau

Colwyn Bay 2009

A lf's new companion at last looked a bit more interested in pursuing the subject now and said, 'Funny, I am here for the very same reason as you.' Again he lied. Still he had no intention of sharing his agenda with a stranger: 'To see if Colwyn Bay has changed much and to try and find the house I lived in for five years and the school I attended. It's not far to come from Liverpool. I have been here often enough, but this time I thought I would look up old haunts.' He didn't want to disclose his real reason for coming here to anyone; it could wait until later, if he were to continue the conversation... or he might just keep it quiet. He had a photo in his wallet. If only he had showed this to Alf.

'*But the town was seriously disrupted; it was never the same again really. I clearly remember the day war broke out...*'

Alf had responded thoughtfully to the comments of his new acquaintance about coming to see if the town had changed (hadn't it just, and no one said it was for the better!), and his desire to look up old haunts. While considering his own many personal memories of his early experiences he said tactfully, '*I am sure our circumstances were completely different. I was a junior clerk in the town's information bureau and one day out of the blue we* had a visit from two civil servants – fairly senior I think – who had been sent from London to make arrangements for the 'Ministry of Food', as it was then, to be evacuated from London to escape the bombings.' 'And… were you able to help them?' asked the stranger, becoming a little intrigued by the story, after all he had lived in this town during the war years. 'In a word – yes,' said Alf, 'so that their department could settle here smoothly. Look around, you, see those hotels, and the blocks of flats where hotels used to stand – they were all turned into offices for the duration of the war, and as it turned out for another three years afterwards. I was in the office on my own at the time, although I was quite young to have such responsibility. I must have been one of the very first to hear about the plans for the town.' He remembered it vividly and related the story to the acquaintance, who seemed interested, and had the time to listen to tales from 1940.

At the Information Bureau. 1940

Bill Owen was in an excited state that morning and preoccupied by events taking place later that day. But professional as ever he gave good service. He turned to his client and handed him a leaflet, one of the remaining few he had left. 'Yes sir, this is the brochure you require. The hotel is on the seafront. Turn right on to the promenade and it's only a hundred yards away. Yes indeed sir, it's a pleasure to help our tourists. If there's anything else we can do please come again.' The bell rang as he left and the door was held open for him by young Alf as the client left and Alf Riley entered. 'Good morning Alf,' said the manager to his young employee. 'Good morning Mr Owen,' answered the trainee. Bill Owen had an urgent question for Alf. 'Can you man the desk this morning? I think you can handle all the tourists' enquiries very competently now, although you have had just a short training. You have picked it up all very quickly. And I expect these days we will be very quiet.'

Alf agreed with him, not expecting too many enquiries that morning. *'Yes, you are right and don't worry, I am sure I can manage, thank you Mr Owen.'* Bill Owen had more news to add.

'Yes, I have a meeting regarding the setting up of the LDV. It's rather important.'

Alf did not know to what he was referring, he had overheard people speaking about the initials, but they had been teasing and saying, *'Look, duck and vanish'* ... so he had to ask, *'What is the LDV?'* Whereupon Owen replied, *'Its Local Defence Volunteers, set up by Anthony Eden. Very important you know. One of the main functions is to guard the coastline, then there's the railway lines to Holyhead... oh and we must keep a look out for parachutists. I fought at Flanders. We all have experience, many of us served in the First World War, others wanted to join but... well they are not really fit enough, and in some cases it was the gas you see. Any men between... oh, about your age and sixty five can join, and I think we can expect thousands, although... there's no pay.'* (By May 14th 250,000 men would sign up in the first 24 hours.) *'But it's weapons we need.'* Alf agreed, *'Yes Mr Owen.'* Owen continued, *'Colonel Fletcher has donated 500 rounds of 12 bore ammunition. But we are going to have to improvise. Davies was the first to volunteer, he has terrible arthritis in his hands but he is still a terrific shot. I expect you will be signing up yourself soon Alf, fine young man like you? I will be sorry to lose you in this office.'* *'Yes sir,'* said Alf. *'I want to join the Navy, to be a telegraphist.'*

'Good man,' replied Owen. Then returning the focus of his thoughts to the present said, *'Well, we don't know if there will be much call for tourists coming in here now at a time like this. I expect it will be quiet.'*

'Really?' said Alf, *'but my uncle said there are people moving into the Llandudno hotels drinking Martinis, playing bridge and reading novels. Planning to stay there until the war ends, they are.'*

Mr Owen said, *'Who could blame them if they can afford it? I would.... mmm Martinis eh? I'll go to the meeting then, you see to these two gentlemen walking in this direction.'* 'Yes sir, of course,' said Alf obediently.

The two men paused outside, deep in conversation then five minutes later the bell above the door rang and two men entered, removing their trilby hats as they crossed the threshold. They were smartly, and expensively dressed. Alf wondered if they were the martini drinking, bridge playing types. He went about his work while they perused some brochures on a stand and a map on the wall, deep in their own thoughts The taller one, moustachioed and dressed in charcoal grey with a fawn mackintosh over his shoulders led the conversation: *'We are in the right place to find out.'* After a short interval Alf thought it was about time he approached them: *'Good morning gentlemen, what can I do for you today?'*

The shorter man introduced them both and got down to business immediately and came out with their reason for being there, which gave Alf quite a shock. *'Yes, young man, my name is Deeves and this is Fillimore here. We are from the Ministry of Food in Whitehall. I am a senior executive officer and Mr Deeves is Head of Branch and we would like to speak to someone in charge. We have identity papers here,'* and produced them with a flourish.

Alf, taken aback, looked at the documents and said, *'Good afternoon sir. And I am Alf. My manager's name is Mr Owen – William Owen. Can I tell him what you are interested in?'* Thinking how beautifully they spoke, they sounded like BBC broadcasters, or stars from some of the films he had recently seen. Not many of his clients spoke with such an accent.

Deeves, impatient for service, wondered why this young boy had been left in charge, but to be fair the Information Bureau staff hadn't been expecting this unannounced visit, and the men were unwilling to wait for the management, impatient.... expecting instant attention like the irritating southerners they were. An official letter had been sent, but the disruption in London had obviously already been on-going for some time. This was a small town, he thought, where nothing ever happened but on first impressions this boy seemed surprisingly efficient, and after all, time was of the essence here. He went on: *'What we have to tell you will be common knowledge shortly, you will know that government departments in London are having difficulty in functioning now that the bombing is intensifying. We need a list of all hotels in the area, and boarding houses too... and how many schools there are, and Public halls and buildings?'*

Alf felt overwhelmed then, and wished Mr Owen had not gone out to his LDV meeting. He would be sorry to miss these men. *'Do you need it right now sir? My manager... he has had to go...'*

Deeves said somewhat impatiently, *'Yes I do... if it's yesterday it's too late! And can I trouble you for a guidebook and a street map please?'*

Alf responded efficiently, *'Yes of course sir. Well sir, there are thirty eight hotels, then there are many more smaller guesthouses here. Most of the churches have their own community halls and there are two large private schools as well as the Grammar school and Central school. Then there are all the junior schools too. I'll just go to fetch the lists, if it's alright with you sir; here are the maps you will need. I will leave you to look at them.'* He handed over two large street maps, and one map of the surrounding areas as well.

Deeves and Fillimore talked aside while Alf fetched details. Maps rustled while he rifled through other papers, surprisingly efficient for his youth and the short time he had worked there, although his fingers shook, his voice sounded confident and belied his nervousness. Deeves, the shorter man, who was less senior, was also smart, but clean-shaven, with a suit not quite as grey, a black overcoat and exceptionally shiny shoes, but was equally as expensively dressed as his colleague. He said privately to Fillimore, *'What do you think of Colwyn Bay? Is it the right choice to bring the Ministry here for goodness knows how long?'*

Fillimore replied, *'But the decision has been made now these plans have been formulating since 1936 when Davenport and Rhondda were in charge, it has been an issue since the last war and we have little choice, other resorts are already receiving some government departments. I believe the Ministry of Agriculture is going to St Anne's on sea and the Inland Revenue to Llandudno. I think about twenty-five thousand civil servants are expected to relocate in all.'*

Fillimore moved his trilby hat away from his briefcase to seek out his notebook and then took his gold fountain pen from his inside pocket. Deeves added, *'Yes, and the Ministry of Education to Bournemouth. It seems that Colwyn Bay is ideal for us, although it is a good distance from London but as it is on the main line from Euston to Holyhead, travelling should not be too bad. The thing is it is going to be a terrific problem housing all our staff in hotels – someone will have the thankless job of telling the owners to clear out their residents and visitors and then all the furniture to make way for our offices and equipment. Thank goodness the requisitioning is someone else's task.'*

He then looked up from the maps, peering above the bifocal spectacles on the end of his nose and said, *'Yes, and see here are the two private boarding schools for boys and for girls, the governors have already been told to look for accommodation away from the area. Yes, we are taking over both – not the junior boys, they can stay, but the older boys will be sent to Oakwood Park in the Conway valley. I believe some of those junior boys could help with various tasks such as the fire watch. What about the girls' school?'*

Fillimore already had information about this. *'Yes the*

headmistress has known for some time that her school will be requisitioned, some of her staff have prepared. The girls will be sent to Chatsworth House in Derbyshire at the invitation of the Duke of Devonshire. It will be a huge disruption, and wear and tear on the house, but not half as much as if the army were to be installed there.'

'Lucky girls,' said Deeves.

Fillimore went on, 'But the girls' school staff have already provided blackout curtains for the whole school building, they came back early from the summer holiday to do so. Trucks have been ordered to take all the furniture, beds and wardrobes to Chatsworth. Do you know they want to take twenty six pianos?'

Deeves became interested in this and said animatedly, 'Really? Yes I know that building, Gilbertsville, wasn't it? It used to be an old spa at one time before it became the school, and it would make an excellent social centre for the Ministry.'

Fillmore quickly agreed to this. 'Yes I agree, better see if we can keep back some pianos then.'

Deeves, setting aside social issues and getting back to the question of the accommodation went on, 'We have to see which of the boarding houses and private homes can take our junior clerks and typists who will have little money to spare. Perhaps we can provide hostels for them.'

Fillmore returned to another problem, which they had briefly touched on earlier. 'The owners of the hotels are not going to like it. But they have to realise there's a war on. Yes we do need a hostel, well... no... two hostels, one for men one for women, to accommodate the single civil servants who will shortly be transferred from the Ministry. I think, let me see... 'Plas Coed' for the women, yes and 'St Enochs' for the men, it's on the promenade and right opposite the largest, grandest, the Colwyn Bay Hotel which may be the centre point of operations here, and headquarters for the whole country. It will free up more room in Whitehall for the cabinet. Then there are the families of these civil servants who are married, some of them have children and they will have to board with the local people. We need to accommodate at least five thousand! And they in turn will be supported by clerks drawn from the local population.'

'Yes, the town is already very crowded with 'Operation Pied Piper' ... the evacuees sent from Liverpool,' said Deeves, looking in his overcoat pocket for his pipe and tobacco. 'I think we should suggest that this town should be restricted from taking any more and what about schooling for the children from the Ministry families? All the schools are full'.

Fillmore cut in here and said, 'What will they say in Bournemouth about that?'

But Deeves tapped his pipe, took out a small soft leather pouch and packed in some St Bruno tobacco then went on. 'So many other problems will be raised, there are so many people wanting to come here for respite from the cities being bombed. We all hope the war won't last too much longer, but who can tell? The Ministry of Food must take priority – we all know how the maintaining of food supplies is such a vital part of the war effort.' He held a match to the bowl of the pipe and sucked until it caught alight and an ember glowed, then he puffed and the aromatic smoke entwined in rising columns.

Alf re-entered the front of the office, rustling papers and saying, 'Here is the list for you sir, all hotels in the town, and this page at the back.' He couldn't help rustling it he was so nervous. 'This is the list of private boarding houses, and also the schools. I have written them down here. Can I help you any further gentlemen?'

'Splendid young man,' said Fillmore, 'that will do for now, but Mr Deeves and I have much to do.'

Alf wondered if he ought to ask but plucked up the courage and boldly ventured a question, after all he would need to tell Mr Owen all about it when he returned. If he didn't say something it may be too late. *'Sir, would you mind if I asked you exactly what is happening?'*

The two men exchanged glances conspiratorially. Deeves sucked on his pipe and a fragrant coil of St Bruno rose twisting in lilac and blue-grey spirals embracing them. Fillmore took a deep breath. There was no harm in explaining to this lad. They would be contacting Owen, his boss, before long with full details. The news would soon be out, especially here in Wales. The word on the street would spread faster than if it were to go into the local paper and people would have time to buffer themselves against the shock and condition themselves to the idea of an *'invasion'* of southerners, so soon after the arrival of the Merseyside children, the soldiers on training exercises and influx of relatives from cities all over the country, but there was not a lot of time.

Fillimore explained, *'Well, I suppose it will not stay a secret for long, most of the public buildings in this town will be taken over... you know... requisitioned. It has been decided that most of our Department – The Ministry of Food – will be evacuated from London to Colwyn Bay – so this will involve a good number of buildings. We are here on a fact-finding mission, and it seems that with your local knowledge we believe you can help us. Many of the civil servants from Whitehall will be arriving within weeks. We shall be setting up a special billeting division in one of the hotels to prepare for the arrival of our staff. Of course there are some of our London staff who don't want to leave their homes – they have their reasons – and whether or not they don't come there will be plentiful opportunities for local people here to take their places. No doubt we will be recruiting among the locals. There is so much to do... clerical and support work. Yes this town will be the headquarters, of course there are other regional offices, but the Minister will be moving here from Whitehall. It's safer here. This town will be completely* disrupted. *And anyway, the space in Whitehall is needed for the Cabinet war office.'*

Deeves suddenly had a brain wave. *'Are you old enough to enlist young man?'*

'No sir,' said Alf disappointedly, *'not until my next birthday.'*

Deeves again drew smoke from his pipe and looked thoughtful, formulating his idea while more St Bruno coursed around the office. *'Well, look here, would you be interested in a job? You seem to have the local knowledge we are looking for, you know where all the buildings are and as for staying in this job... there will be no room for tourists in this town, there will be a job for your mother too as we need an army of clerks. There are food offices set up all over the country to deal with the rationing, but here in this town will be the headquarters. Food is a vital weapon in war you know.'*

Alf was flattered, and beamed broadly. He really must have done well this morning. Mr Owen would be pleased with him when he returned. But not if he thought he was going to desert this office for another job. But Owen was expecting him to enlist soon anyway. Alf thought, he had to do what was most useful for the war effort, and it was true he did have lots of local knowledge. *'Well thank you sir, yes I would be very interested in working with you if you think I could help, since am not yet old enough to join the navy. But I shouldn't think my mother will apply, she runs a boarding house, and she is busy looking after her visitors.'*

Deeves seemed delighted. *'Splendid young fellow. When can you start?'*

Alf was stunned, what would his parents say? And furthermore, what would Mr Owen say? He was so wrapped up in the LDV he would hardly notice Alf's absence. Little did Alf know this would be the start of a great career for him in the civil service. *'Well, thank you sir, but I will have to speak to Mr Owen*

*when he comes back from the LDV meeting. But you know where to
find me when you need me'.*

Fillimore picked up his overcoat from the bentwood coat
stand where it hung, he was ready to go. He was thinking that
they could go for a whisky at the Imperial, before having lunch
at their hotel, '*The Cartmell*,' the '*businessmen's hotel*' on Station
Road. Deeves was pleased with the way things had gone today
and the plans, which had been embryonic since 1936 were now
well under way. Food shortages during and after the last war had
weakened the population, that would not happen again.

* * *

Alf finished his story, something he hadn't discussed with
anyone for years. No one had been interested before in hearing
it. He had wondered how this listener would respond, would he
reciprocate with his own story?

'*What a contrast to me,*' said the younger man, who was
actually 76, but several years younger than Alf. '*I was just a six
year old sent here from a poor part of Liverpool and dumped on an
unsuspecting family, the Joneses. They were very good to me and me
brother and sister, but I longed to get back home. Many of us evacuees
were so homesick some did return to Liverpool during the war',* he
paused meaningfully, '*with tragic consequences.'*

Alf looked thoughtful, taking in what this man had meant
by that, and then after a respectable interval went on
enthusiastically, since he thought he had found someone with
enthusiasm and a depth of interest unusual these days. '*I got
involved with the billeting of the civil servants who were all ages and
some were trade advisors for various foodstuffs. This was only for a
short while because I was drafted into the navy. You see homes had to
be provided for the evacuated staff and although some places could be*

found it became necessary to issue billeting notices on any local residents who had rooms to spare. This caused some ill feeling...'

'Yes, understandably,' said the man in the sweater, remembering a mix of people of all types when he had lived there as a child.

Alf continued: *'Because the notice required the residents to provide accommodation, breakfast and an evening meal every day for just one guinea a week. Ridiculous really – that's why the civil servants were called...'* he laughed out loud, '*"guinea pigs"*. It all *settled down eventually and those who could paid a bit extra.'*

CHAPTER 4

Return to retro recipes

Colwyn Bay 1992

'No weapon ever invented is more deadly than hunger, it can spike guns, destroy courage and break the will of the most resolute peoples.'
Land at War 1939 – 1944 HMSO 1945

Faye was preparing a meal in the kitchen. It was not a complicated menu, but all went smoothly, Beryl was a great help, she couldn't have wished for a more fantastic mother-in-law, who was not only a great cook (she had even run a restaurant feted in Colwyn Bay in her younger days), but she contributed without interfering and they just got on like a house on fire. Faye felt very fortunate, and Beryl thought her daughter-in-law very easy going too, so they were both well suited. Beryl was approachable and had a great sense of humour, and of all her four children Faye thought her husband resembled her the most. The family liked traditional food, well all food really, except the grandson of five years old, who liked junk food. Faye and her husband couldn't believe he was their son because he was so fussy, whereas they liked everything. They had been brought up with different influences, there was still rationing until 1954, therefore austerity, and had been no foreign influences so there had not been the choices there were in the 90s. People didn't holiday abroad in the 1950s, they went to the British seaside.

Faye had learned to cook a fair amount from her own mother, and then when away from home at college and when she found a job and lived in a flat in the '70s one of her favourite cookbooks was written by Marguerite Patten, 'Food for Families' and 'Food for working wives', although at the time she was not married, but she was definitely working, and liked to prepare food for dinner before she left for her job in the morning. She had picked up a copy of a Marguerite Patten book of wartime recipes aptly called 'We'll eat again' and couldn't wait to show it to Beryl.

'Look,' said Faye, '"dried eggs". I have heard about that from my mum, she had a poem about them... and "steamed fish roll", "fish charlotte",' she wrinkled her nose at this thought. 'Then "pigs in clover"?' Her voice lilted upward questioningly and she raised her eyebrows. 'None of these recipes are in Jamie Oliver's book, and there are some things here I'd like to recreate, like corned beef rissoles. What is "American mince?" And it tells you all sorts of things in here like what the rations were, how much you got and how the ration books worked. It must have been very difficult in those days. There must have been lots of things in this book that you remember cooking.'

'Of course I do,' said Beryl. 'But I was only a young girl then, so I didn't do much cooking, but I remember eating them. I was at school when the war started. I lived above the hairdressers with my mother on Station Road.'

'Yes,' said Faye, 'I remember Nanny, I only met her once.'

Beryl went on reminiscing. 'My father had died by then, he had TB. It was rife in those days and we had moved away from Manchester to North Wales because of the wonderful health benefits. The sea air was good for him. He slept in a tent in the garden when *we lived in Llysfaen so that he could fully benefit from the clean sea air. But although it didn't save him and he still died, it must have prolonged his life.'*

Faye looked thoughtful at the memories of her son's great grandfather, so thankful that the family had relocated from Manchester in those days, because otherwise she may never have met her husband, the love of her life. Then returning to the subject of the town during wartime, said: *'So, it must have been fairly quiet here during the war, you wouldn't have felt at risk here in the north, well not in Colwyn Bay would you?'*

'At risk, no,' said Beryl, *'although we were under the flight path from Liverpool, and there were a few bombs jettisoned. But quiet?'* Beryl laughed, *'No indeed, it was not, it was a different place altogether in those days. The Ministry of Food was here you know.'*

'Really?' said Faye. *'That would be the regional office then?'*

'Oh no, indeed not', said Beryl. 'It was the headquarters for the whole country, and Lord Woolton was here – he lived at the Station Hotel at the Junction, but it was the Colwyn Bay Hotel on the prom which was the main headquarters, where he had his office.'

Faye was amazed. *'I remember that building before it was knocked down and flats were built in its place.'*

'Yes,' said Beryl, sighing sadly; *'the town was never the same after the war, and that hotel... it was so grand, it had a maze of corridors on the lower ground floor, and it was set up for ladies arriving with their maids. At the time it was built this resort was a very elegant place to holiday, so genteel... how times change, the town has a different character and everyone wants to go abroad these days. Anyway, during wartime all the hotels in the town were taken over by the Ministry... thirty-eight of them, and the two private schools as well. It was never the same again.'*

'Well, I can hardly believe it,' said Faye. *'I grew up here and no one ever mentioned it before, and it is fascinating to imagine it, but of*

course although I was born here, my parents were not here during wartime, they met in Cumbria while my Dad was training with the RAF.' She suddenly realised he must have enlisted from here, from Colwyn Bay while he worked as an insurance agent.

'Five thousand civil servants suddenly arrived,' it was all coming back to Beryl now, she was enjoying talking about it, and reliving her memories; *'and of course they all had to be housed. But even that was not enough staff to do all the administration; they had to recruit clerks among the local people. Many of them were housewives who hadn't worked before, and the Ministry even went to the schools and recruited among school leavers, fifteen year olds.'*

'I am amazed,' Faye said thoughtfully. She wanted to know more. *'I am going to the library tomorrow to see what else I can find out'.*

'Do you think Alex would like to go?' said Beryl.

'I shouldn't think so,' answered Faye, *'he would much rather play with his Game-Boy or watch a video, but I will take him anyway.'*

Beryl continued. *'There are a lot of people still around who could tell you about it... it's just that no one ever asks about those days, we didn't think anyone was interested.'* She opened the oven and brought out a baking tray of beautifully risen golden sponge buns. She was going to make 'butterflies' with whipped cream for her grandson. He loved them. *'Just think, in this batch there would have been one person's whole allowance of butter for a week in wartime,'* Beryl wistfully told her daughter-in-law. *'I don't know how our mothers managed.'*

Back in wartime the typical weekly food allowance had varied from month to month as food gradually became more and more scarce. To begin with in 1940 only, bacon, butter and sugar were rationed. Those women queuing would have been despondent if they had realised that rationing would not end entirely until way into the unimaginable future, 1954.

Early one morning in 1940 outside 'Evans and Davies', the small grocery shop, the women who had registered there queued with baskets over their arms; some had brought newspapers with them in order to wrap the produce. The queue grew longer by the minute and the shop had just opened, but there was no alternative because that was the only place they could get goods since they were registered there. It had taken a while for shoppers and retailers alike to become accustomed to the new system of having their cards marked when they obtained goods, and cutting out the coupons and in the constantly fluctuating availability and procedures patience was of the essence.

Those near the front were lucky enough to hear in the recesses of the shop sounds of a till ringing, a good sign then, there were provisions to be had, and there was muted conversation. They had all received their latest ration books recently and were anxious to get out and claim their entitlements. Two of these housewives queuing were the same two women friends who had talked on the day war broke out on the way home from church, they were now pleased to meet up again after a busy interval and chat together in the queue, giving each other updates on their progress, and hoping for a bit of a quiet gossip.

Olwen had beamed when she had seen her friend Jenny in the queue. She had had an exhausting morning already, having been up since six to light the fire, to sweep, dust and polish, then serve all the residents in her boarding house with breakfast and do the washing up. She had sent her children to school, tended her vegetable garden and was by nine ready for a little company, conversation and diversion. Jenny may have some news for her. She greeted her warmly.

'Hello Jenny, have you got your new ration books there? I have mine, they came this morning, and also a letter giving notice that now we are all to take evacuees... not that I have any room left.'

Jenny certainly did have news. 'Yes I do have the books, and I have some news for you. I have been so busy, that's why we haven't seen each other in so long. Well, would you believe it? I do have some evacuees! I have three children from Liverpool... mind you, I only wanted one little girl to go to school with my daughter but these three were left without anywhere to go, and there was nothing else for it. As usual far more arrived on the train than they ever expected. It happens every time. How those Voluntary Service women cope I just don't know. My husband Emlyn had to bring them home. I wasn't too pleased at first I can tell you. Emlyn was in the doghouse'.

Olwen was amazed. 'Really? Well, after all, what else could Emlyn do? And how are they getting on?

Jenny Jones looked around her circumspectly. You never knew who was listening next to you, and she had noted well those posters 'Careless Talk' with a picture of Hitler saying 'Mr Hitler wants to know... silence makes him simply Fuehrious' and all that. It had changed her life, because she had always enjoyed a good craic. So in a quiet voice she said, 'Nice enough children, but we had to give them a good wash if you know what I mean.' She sniffed disdainfully. 'And they had hardly any clothes with them, so the WVS are helping there...'

Olwen nodded sympathetically, but Jenny had much more to say. 'And the children are Catholics. I can tell you, their parents are not happy about them going to our school. The nuns came round to check up on us. They had told their parents that I was being cruel to them. But Olwen,' she said plaintively, 'I only give them the same good discipline as my own daughter!'

Olwen reassured her supportively in soothing tones, 'Well of course Jenny, everyone knows you are a very respectable family.'

Jenny, relieved at the confidence Olwen had in her, sniffed again and said smiling, *'Yes... thank you.'* Then looking round again furtively, to see if they were being overheard she went on: *'On the first night I went to see if they were comfortable in bed after their bath and I found them **under** the bed. Well, at first I thought they were worried about bombs but no it wasn't that... and when I asked them what they were doing under there they said to me "this is where we sleep at home".'*

Now Olwen was genuinely shocked and began to be secretly relieved that she was fully occupied with soldiers and civil servants, and unable to have taken any evacuees after all and came out with it. *'Whatever they are like, I am afraid I cannot take in any children under any circumstances, I am full up. And I can't even take any of my regular boarders who come here every year because I already have so many civil servants who have not been able to get into the two hostels. I get a guinea a week each for them, which is little enough as I have to give them all their meals, and with rationing that is difficult. Lucky we are encouraged to "Dig for Victory" and to cultivate the lawn and flowerbeds with vegetables; I tell you, those runner beans are a godsend.'*

The local park had been dug up and planted as allotments in response to a report in the local paper on 20th June 1940. A councillor had spoken out and the headline had been 'Cut the red tape'. There had been a furore. He wanted to 'Protect the people and take steps to ensure food cultivation'; also he suggested that roadmen should be making the terrain impossible for enemy planes to land without being crippled.

'Every fit man and woman should be compelled to do something in this time of peril.' He went on: *'It was no time for kid-glove methods. They could not fight ruthlessness with "dope" and soothing syrup.'* There had been a growing impatience with the futilities of the council. Some things don't change. In an interview after

the meeting the councillor had questioned the growing of flowers by fourteen gardeners and suggested that schoolchildren could be growing food. It must have had an effect. The park was now planted with varieties of vegetables.

Jenny agreed with Olwen regarding the taking on of the civil servants. *'Yes better to take the "Guinea pigs", because if you do take evacuees you know you would only get a few shillings for each of them. And another thing; do you know the schools are so full, what with all the Ministry children as well, they have to operate a shift system! How those teachers cope I just don't know.'*

Olwen sighed. *'Yes, one of my lodgers, head of 'Butter and Cheese' he is, has a daughter at the County school, Miranda Elliot, she's a lovely girl. Sixteen she is... but...* (lowering her voice) *she does seem a lot older.'*

Jenny passed on the news that she had heard. *'They say they are going to build more temporary buildings as classrooms in the grounds of the County School, like we had in the first war, prefabricated, so they can get them in use quickly. And did you hear of the private school children ? they have gone **already**, buildings are needed for the Ministry.'* She noted Olwen's shocked expression and went on imparting information. *'Well the boys have gone to Oakwood Park, that big country house down the Valley, that is... all except the junior boys, **they** can stay in **their** building. Some of them are employed in fire watching with the Ministry workers, so they're useful they are.'*

Olwen asked, *'And what about the girls from the other school?'*

Jenny knew all about that too. *'Well, they have gone to Chatsworth House in Derbyshire. The Duke of Devonshire invited them as his guests! At least those young ladies will not be as much wear and tear on the house as it would be if the army were using it, with their big boots. But it is not really luxury there for them; I mean, no four poster beds, they use the dining room and state rooms as a* dormitories, and they would have to keep to the usual rules... like not using too much water. They too can have only one bath a week, and then only five inches of water... and they also have to do their own washing up!'

Olwen looked on thoughtfully for a minute then commented on the situation of the girls of the private school. *'I didn't say anything to you before, but I think the headmistress here must have known something about this some time ago. We saw all the lorries taking away the furniture, beds, pianos the lot... there were twenty, no maybe thirty of them going back and forth all day. I heard that the staff came back early from the summer holidays and made sateen blackout curtains for the whole building, so the Ministry was lucky that was already in place. I heard it will be a social club for all the Civil Servants. There are thousands of them here and more yet to come from London. Mind you, I don't know where they will all live.'*

'Who told you that? Jenny was quick to ask.

'Well,' said Olwen, looking around her cautiously, *'Well, as it's you... I'll tell you. You know my husband is working at the information bureau, well his assistant, Alf, he has now gone to work with the civil servants. They came to get the information about all the buildings available.'*

'Is that right Olwen? said Jenny. *'Well there are no hotels free, they are all becoming offices, I saw them moving all the beds and wardrobes out of "The Metropole Hotel" and depositing them in that large warehouse past the west end. Then they brought rolls and rolls of brown lino and filing cabinets as far as the eye could see!'*

The queue moved up, they were nearly at the front now. Jenny had another question for Olwen. *'There must be plenty of work at the Ministry, tell me is your daughter applying for work?'*

'Yes, Jenny, but not at the Ministry, I know some of her friends have applied. No she's not, she is going to be a machine operator in the diamond factory.'

Jenny was mystified at this, saying, '*Well! Even though there is a war on I have seen a lot of advertisements in the paper for fur coats, at Rosie Davis' shop, but I did not know anything about diamonds?*' She was flabbergasted at the idea that people were frivolous enough to think of jewellery and furs during wartime, but this had been a premiere shopping area before the war, drawing elite clients from a wide area, and now the wealthy from cities were drawn to the town as a peaceful haven, free from bombing.

Olwen answered Jenny informatively. '*Yes, you see the furs are being remodelled, and they say "scientifically cleaned" there are no coupons needed you see, and the diamonds? Well, they are not for jewellery now, they are for tools. I have some Belgian workers as my lodgers, and their manager too, that's how we got my daughter her job. My husband doesn't want her joining the Wrens or going away.*'

Jenny was genuinely fascinated now and wanted to know more. '*What tools are they making with the diamonds?*' she asked.

Olwen replied, '*Navigation instruments for planes. There are other factories on the coast starting up too. My daughter says it's horribly noisy in the factory when the machines are going. There was a new machine expected from America, but the ship it was being carried on was torpedoed, and a replacement is coming, as soon as it gets here she can start work then.*' Olwen became distracted. '*Oh Good... the queue is moving. Jenny, is it sugar you want today?*'

'*Yes I do, well everything really, it's hard to feed so many people with so little. Emlyn caught some mackerel yesterday; he was fishing off the pier... It all helps. And do you know they have taken off some planks in case of enemy landings?*'

Olwen was appalled. '*No Jenny, it's not deep enough for any boats to land, unlike Rhos Pier I can see the sense in that!*'

'*But did you hear about the funeral coming out of Anglesey?*'

Now Olwen could find out something, and eager for information asked: '*No, whose was it? What happened?*'

'*Well,*' said Jenny, relishing the chance to pass on this bit of gossip, '*there was obviously something suspicious going on, and when they insisted on opening the coffin they found it was full of butter.*'

Olwen was aghast, '*No... it's "spivs" we call them, who profiteer from shortages. What a scandal! And we are only allowed four ounces each person per week, and that is either butter or lard for everything, cooking and all. How will we manage? Only four ounces of bacon too. I have heard that some who breed pigs hide an extra one now and again. We all have to do our bit, and cheating is scandalous, so Lord Woolton says.*'

'*Woolton?*' said Jenny?

'*Yes, he is the Minister of Food now, he replaced Morrison,*' said Olwen. '*And he lives at the Station Hotel at Llandudno Junction. Did you see that item in the paper, he compared the cheats to worms! It was Food Education week last Wednesday and he spoke at the exhibition, it was in the paper, look I have it here. '* Olwen produced a copy of the local paper from her shopping basket, the newspaper which she had brought to wrap up her provisions, and pointed at the article. Jenny produced her glasses from her basket, put them on and read out loud.

'Lord Woolton's final warning' it said in large letters, then the subtitle 'To Gamblers in food', comparing them to worms. '*These people,*' he said, '*must remember that I know something about commercial life, and that I am watching them. This is the last warning they will get. After all what is the use of making a little extra money out of food? It is not going to be of any use to these people unless we win this war and they are not helping us. They are in fact putting us to an immense amount of trouble and cost and the nation does not need to have any more cost to bear. Why are they allowed to exist? Because they are like the worms of the earth, they slither along and go underground.*'

Other women in the queue were taking note, and expressed

their approval, since Olwen and Jenny had dropped their conspiratorial hush and resumed their normal tone, forgetting about the 'careless talk' momentarily.

'Yes that applies all over the country,' said Olwen. 'I remember there wasn't much to eat when we were children in the last war, and it was illegal to waste food. Oh yes you can still be fined now even if you are caught putting scraps in the bin instead of feeding it to the pigs.' Both women were youngsters between 1914 and 1918. 'But I think now there are towns far worse off than we are, it's not only lack of food.'

Jenny couldn't agree more: 'Olwen, You are so right. Did you see the sky over Liverpool last night? It was red with fire. We all stood on the promenade and watched it. Then I thought how lucky that all these children have been sent here, bless them.'

Olwen was philosophical. 'None of us know what to expect, after all we are under the flight path from France to Liverpool, and there are often bombs jettisoned in the fields.'

This was something Jenny did know about. 'My daughter was sent home from her guide meeting the other day, and there was a dog fight going on in the sky above the fields between the guide hall and our house, poor lamb, she was terrified when she arrived home. Well how foolish of the guide leader to send her home and not keep her in the hall. I still think that all the civil servants are lucky to be away from London in this lovely place. Mind you it was more peaceful before the war, not so crowded. Yes, Olwen, they are lucky, but they complain about our small town ways. We do all try to get on, after all there is a war on. I am so glad to have met you here today, as they don't tell us as much on the newsreels do they? Who knows what else is happening.'

CHAPTER 5

Butter, Cheese and Diamonds

Spring 2009

Muriel assembled yet another folding cardboard packing case and fighting the instinct to stop and have a third cup of tea and switch on the daytime TV game shows, she returned to her task with a sigh. She had constantly kept on top of the situation, or so she thought, she had tried to keep her possessions under control. Her house had always been tidy, not obsessively so, but relatively uncluttered compared to others. The acquisitive instinct had declined as she had aged, but having by now reached her mid-eighties, she had already collected a disproportionate number of possessions and mementoes which she had loved having around her, as well as gifts which she was obliged to keep. Everything she touched had a magical memory for her and as she hovered over them like a human cursor memories popped up afresh in 'mental bubbles'. As much as it broke her heart to give away such items, or worse to bin them (well the bin was more than full now anyway despite the county's excellent disposal services) she felt glad and thankful that she herself was fit enough to carry out this job herself and not leaving it to her family to do after she was gone. She knew from her own experience what a poignant task it could be. Now she could dispose appropriately with things. Others, she had heard, had relatives who when they died had hired a skip and tossed in the precious along with the junk, forced to choose the present over the past and perhaps because they had to act quickly and return to their homes, their work and responsibilities in other towns, or was it too painful to dwell on what was left of their relatives' lives? In many cases they later sadly regretted the irreversibility of their actions.

This house had been her family home with her husband, until he had died of cancer. Sadly her daughter had been quite young at the time. Herbert had died here in this house with Muriel looking after him; he hadn't wanted to go into hospital. Then afterwards she and her daughter Millie had stayed and lived on there, being able to afford this through her career in administration.

Millie, having lost her father had found solace in her schoolwork and had studied hard for her university place, wanting to emulate her mother's work ethic and to make her (and even the ghost of her late father) proud. Millie was inspired to find meaning in her work, achieving her ambition to be a doctor. She lived nearby with her own family now. Her daughter Grace had not had Millie's character. Shallow and vain, always thinking about herself, or pop music and the culture of celebrity. Not entirely her fault, what with all the media pressure. She had a dream and desperately wanted to be a singer in a band, which was fine for a hobby, but who knew if she was really good enough to rely on it as a career, and as for the clothes she wore, Muriel had despaired, as had every generation about the apparel of its offspring.

Muriel picked up a framed photograph of her granddaughter Grace as a pretty little girl; she had been such a lovely baby. What happened? and then things changed... they got worse before they got better... things had calmed down these days. She had seemed to grow up quickly. Muriel had had a hand in this while her daughter and son-in-law were busy with their careers the teenager had spent a lot of time with her grandmother. Time and attention was what she most needed, not material possessions. *'Oh well,'* Muriel thought, scolding herself for digressing from her focus, *'this won't buy the proverbial baby a new bonnet.'* And she got back to work. Her next thought was, *'What would happen to all the oil paintings she had done over the years?'*

Then there were all these files from her family's college days, file upon file from Millie's medical training and even going back to school days, Millie could take them to her house and defer the decision to discard. There were school reports of her husband's from the local school here in Colwyn Bay, it was then called the *County School*. The reports were attached through holes at the corner with silver tipped green cords just like the civil service used. In addition there was a box of pen nibs and a dried up bottle of ink, at which she mused, how did they ever managed with these primitive implements in her Civil Service days, they couldn't afford to make any mistakes or waste any time. Wouldn't people today have been incredulous? If only they had had the benefit of modern technology to carry out their work; to have the luxury of a computer with spreadsheets to do the adding up, and an *undo button* if they made a mistake, email instead of the telephone which had to be queued for – although she was never allowed to use it – but they all managed, and managed very well indeed in their important work.

Turning aside the nibs and ink she spied a box of commemorative coins. Perhaps she should go on one of those programmes, *be on a show*, where they find the *'treasure'* and sell it for you achieving funds for particular purposes. No she would have hated it, she was much too private a person and needed to do this herself. Actually she felt glad she had embarked on the task before any of her relatives had called in one of those teams to transform the house, she valued her familiar surroundings and her independence, and with the help of a very good cleaner who skirted around the accumulated items, and fetched some shopping for her she continued to run her home herself.

After the third and fourth cups of tea and a quick look at the local paper she got back stuck in to her task. She had noted the newspaper report of the knife attack at the local garage, it was not the first time that place had been a target: '*Things have changed so much*' she thought sadly, '*I wouldn't feel safe going out at night*'.

Trying to focus on the task in hand she went back to looking through the drawers of the desk. Now then! What was this? A diary? but not hers, she had forgotten where she had put this item, and now it had come to light in the old bureau. It had belonged to her late husband's father who had been in the trenches in the First World War, and this leather bound notebook was his record of his time in France until 1919. It was an unassuming book, like its owner, whom she remembered affectionately.

Grace perused the pages briefly, again allowing herself to be distracted. It was written by Percy in a casual and functional manner in fading pencil and in an elegant hand. She knew there were reports of casualties, men he had fought alongside killed in front of him, and then you would have to read between the lines. But here was at least one cheerful entry. Her eyes rested on Christmas Day 1918.

'*Breakfast as usual. Helped cooks all morning peeling spuds etc. Dinner up as usual about 2pm. There was a good feed of turkey and vegetables, pudding, etc. followed by beer rum punch, cigars and cigarettes, fruit etc. Brigadier looked in during dinner and made a little speech. Cheers were given by the Brigadier, Staff Captain and the signal officer. Sing song followed dinner which lasted until about 5 o'clock. Left about 5.30pm and went into town with Sharp and Powell. Had some drink and then went to cinema. Not much good the explanatory part being in German, but the music was splendid.'*

Of course 1918, they had advanced into Germany. Later she noticed, *'Troops talk of nothing else but demobilisation now.'* She would read this later, she would go back to the part where they were in France and under heavy shelling attack. He was lucky to come home, there were incidents all the way through describing loss of life and injury. The writer had been only nineteen when he had enlisted, fearless, invincible yet the pages mentioned the casualties by name among the listed timetable of events. It was written unemotionally, otherwise how could he have gone on?

'What a valuable resource this could be for an historian,' thought Muriel, *'who could she pass it on to?'* There was no local museum where she could hand in this treasure for safekeeping, there was one in Llandudno, but this diarist had been a local man, born here in the 1890s and he would have wanted it kept where it belonged. However, what if it had gone unnoticed slipped in to the skip with less important documents? Then it would be gone for ever. She shuddered, horrified to think that this had happened already, so often in so many cases. And what was here of hers besides the oil paintings? She kept her own diary in a box under the bed, but in addition the memories she had not written down were locked away in her mind. She often thought of her early days and they had seemed to become more vivid as she had got older, whereas she sometime forgot more recent events. She reflected what was the most important thing she had done in her life – well, obviously, begetting and bringing up her daughter of course and looking after her husband in his final

illness. Yes that was it. But in her younger days she had worked, she had not expected to ever get a job in administration when she was growing up in the 1920s and '30s yet being in the right place at the right time she had contributed in her way to the war effort in the 1940s by working in the distribution of butter and cheese for the whole country, not in the same way as her father-in-law in the Great War of course, he had risked his life.

But she too had done her bit. In return the training she had received during that opportunity to contribute to war work had changed her life and given her a career and a route out of this town, albeit temporarily. She remembered the day she had gone for the interview, in 1940, full of trepidation, her memories now drifted vividly into 1940...

Colwyn Bay 1940

Before setting out on her bus journey on that morning in the early days of the war Muriel Thomas had changed into her best outfit. 'Best' such as it was, she had few clothes other than her school uniform, but her mother was good with a needle and had taught Muriel to be the same – needs must. The pale pink flowered liberty printed *tea* frock which had been handed down from a more affluent relative had been cut down imaginatively and no one would have recognised it. Superlative home dressmaking skills saved Muriel from embarrassment, not that there was any stigma attached to wearing used clothing then. The rationing of clothing would not start until December 1941, but for many the limitations were financial then, even before coupons were initiated.

Muriel took a deep breath and walked purposefully but apprehensively towards the Metropole Hotel, in the centre of

Colwyn Bay, where she was to apply for work. It was a grand building central to the town. She had often looked across at it but had as yet never been inside. In her imagination she could see the horse drawn carriages waiting outside as they had in her grandparents' day, bringing the 'toffs' here for visits when it was newly built, she had seen the pictures. Four storeys high, the handsome red brick building fronted on to both Penrhyn Road and Princes Drive, with a clock tower on the corner.

As she approached the stained glass canopied entrance, she noticed a figure standing, just gazing at the building and wondered if this person was also looking for employment as she was. There was something bizarre about her clothing, the cut of the jacket was unusual, it was the skirt length – and the shoes a very uncommon shape with heels higher than Muriel had ever seen. The woman's hair was worn loose, very long, dark and silky and she carried a smart soft leather case.

Although she studied the building intently she seemed not to see Muriel at all, and more strangely she had a brooch on her lapel, and she seemed to be talking towards it, no not really a brooch more like her grandfather's watch on a chain. How odd. There were all sorts of strange people here these days from all over, with their different ways. Muriel wondered if she could be a *foreigner*, you could never be too careful.

Eventually she generously gave her the benefit of the doubt, after all she hadn't heard her speak, didn't know whether she spoke English, Welsh or a foreign language, and speculated that maybe she too was nervous and was practising what she was going to say at her interview. Muriel then passed her and went up a few shallow steps through a door with gleaming polished brass handles, looking over her shoulder smiling, to see if the woman was following or whether she should hold the door open for her. Strangely she had completely disappeared and Muriel could not even see her anywhere on the street she had just vanished, so she wasn't coming to seek employment after all, and Muriel was thinking, 'We all have to struggle to give ourselves confidence', but ought she to mention it to someone?

She decided to keep well out of it and went inside finding herself in a hallway opposite a ballroom. Although she had never been in here before she had always imagined it, but once over the threshold she suffered a sudden and unexpected disappointment as the grandeur diminished somewhat. The newly requisitioned hotel seemed in partial chaos amid all the crowded rows of metal filing cabinets with a few desks and old wooden tables hastily lined up on the brown lino, not at all what she had expected.

Muriel overcame her shattered illusions, spoke to the receptionist and was signalled to sit down on one of the chairs in a corridor where there were several other women waiting, she imagined by their approximate age and appearance that some were housewives also interested in a clerical job, but she didn't recognise anyone In the hurriedly makeshift offices there was the echoing sound of an old-fashioned typewriter going clickety-click with the bell ringing out at intervals each time the carriage returned.

Muriel sat for a while before another young lady, somewhat older than herself, with beautifully coiffured hair wandered in. She was dressed in a fawn suit, carrying a tan leather handbag and a newspaper. After speaking to the receptionist she then sat next to Muriel, opened her paper and started to read the small ads. Muriel could not help but notice that she was searching through the accommodation section. 'Houses to let or wanted,' she could read over the woman's expensively suited fawn elbow. There was also an advert for employment, 'Well paid war work for women. You can help the men in the defence services and have a *good job in the N.A.F.F.I. canteen in any one of the following positions Cooks from 24/9 per week then counter assistants and kitchen maids from 16/6 per week.'* That seemed like a lot of money to Muriel. She hoped the woman could not feel her eyes peering over to furtively share the paper. The woman uncomfortably shifted her position slightly so that another section was visible further down the page.

'Unfurnished accommodation wanted by government official, Exchange modern six room house', then all that was to be seen was *'wanted, wanted, wanted'...* right down to the end of the page. The woman sighed and closed the paper, looking despondent. She had seen the Public notices that morning in the Weekly News.

There was an appeal by the mayor to all householders in the borough of Colwyn Bay. He had said: *'I am sure all residents will appreciate the necessity of completing this removal – the further transfer of more civil servants – the authorities are particularly anxious to obtain the cheerful co-operation of everybody in this task, I appeal to all to render service to their country by taking in the maximum number they can accommodate so that the necessity for compulsory billeting shall not arise. I feel sure that all of us realise that the task has to be faced, that the Civil Servants are leaving their own homes to come her because their duty demands it, and that they will form part of our community until victory is achieved. It is up to us all to assist to the utmost of our ability and I feel confident that the people of Colwyn Bay will rise to the occasion.'* The paper was dated Thursday June 27th 1940.

In a room out of sight, a dark blue grosgrain tailored jacket with a marcasite lapel pin adorning the collar was carefully placed over the back of a chair. On the table in front of it was a huge stack of files bulging in manila folders. The jacket belonged to one of the civil servants transferred from Whitehall to carry out her duty in an area entirely new to her. Frances

Harrington, born and bred in Guildford, strutted in her shiny highly polished heels. She was in her forties and a single lady with an elaborately '*amami*' waved hairstyle, she had availed herself of the services of the hairdresser, Russell's, on Station Road that very morning before work, as was customary on a regular basis to beautify her glossy chestnut tresses. She had no intention of dropping her standards even if she was in this small town where, to her dismay, from what she had seen so far, women did not seem to attach as much importance to glamour as in the Southern counties and cities. While Frances looked extremely chic, at the same time she meant business. She wore a double row of graduated pearls with a sapphire clasp around her swanlike neck and was dressed immaculately in a dark blue slim line skirt and a crisp white blouse topped with a dark blue cardigan of cashmere.

After her very good private education in the South of England Frances had worked at the Ministry for years, knowing herself destined to be a career woman. She had lost her sweetheart during the Great War, he had never returned from the trenches and since then she had never met another man, nor wanted to, and instead devoted her life to her career. She had not risen very high in the ranks; those positions were reserved for the men. There were of course fewer men around now as many had enlisted, but her male colleagues were classified as being in a '*reserved occupation*' so the chances of her promotion were remote.

She was a capable woman and efficient but rarely had she had such a demanding task as this, it tested her to fill so many clerical positions in such a short time. No telephone lines, few typewriters and hardly any paper and vitally all departments needed manpower, or now it was to be also 'woman power'. There had been a queue of applicants after the positions had been advertised in the local paper, but it fell to her to assess their skills and administer the tests, and she needed good accurate reliable staff and for so many departments, so many buildings. The administrative task of manning them was to be overwhelming, but there was no margin for failure. There was a list of all departments for example 'Butter and Cheese' then there was the 'Meat division' as well as 'Bacon and Ham' then 'Cereals' and the 'Bread Division'. 'Animal foodstuffs' was equally important and so many more and all of these had managers in charge of ordering from all over the world and transferring to storage and distribution all over the country. This particular aspect of war work was vital, but then it was *all* vital, and how long was this to go on for?

She was doing her bit. At the moment there were plenty of administrators, staff transferred from Whitehall, but so many managers, and no one to do the extensive mundane but essential clerical and accounting work. '*Too many chiefs and no Red Indians*', some had said. The middle managers had come in droves, with their wives and families in tow, an influx of at least five thousand employees in to a town of a population of twenty thousand maximum. The town had increased by twenty five per cent overnight! Some of the new arrivals had not been terribly pleased with their accommodation, but since it was so scarce they were lucky to have any places and had to make do. The single people had been in hostels, one for men and one for women, but the families had had to take rooms in lodging houses and some in private homes where the local wives would cook for them from the combined meagre rations.

But there were some pluses, safety for one thing. Also, they loved the seaside with its sweeping sandy bay, mountains as a backdrop and open green spaces. The clean sea air was bracing and it brought roses to their cheeks replacing their 'London pallor'. Although the local population had stared in disbelief and were initially very wary of these 'invaders' they had come with a purpose for the common good and co-operation was paramount, not optional. Shopkeepers had welcomed them and the high-class ladies outfitters had thought, what a relief, they may be able to remain open and keep their livelihood to cater to these career women and the wives of the top brass civil servants.

Frances was lodging in the Owen guesthouse, a short walk from work, no train journey such as she had experienced in Guildford. It was clean and comfortable enough and Olwen Owen although unsophisticated was a good woman, a plain cook and a pleasant enough woman, devout and working hard at serving her family and all her guests. Frances paid a guinea a week. It was the Elliot family who had introduced her to her landlady, they lodged there too, and she had known them in the south. There were some soldiers, and also one or two Belgian men who ran a factory, manufacturing diamond tools for navigation instruments. She didn't know what they paid for their accommodation. She occasionally practised her school French in conversation with them, but did not socialise with them. After her busy work schedule she sometimes went to the Civil Servants' Penrhos college social club and met up with some of the people from Guildford, and so many others from the south. There were really so many people, some that you had never seen before and some you were never likely to meet again. There was plenty of company about, but Frances preferred her nights to be early. She would look forward to curling up with a good book and a hot drink at bedtime.

Frances took her steel rimmed glasses from the leather pouch and put them on the end of her elegant aristocratic nose and looked down her list, running a pale pink painted fingernail down the page. She then looked up and through the open door of her room at the row of women sitting on chairs in the corridor outside her office. She smiled welcomingly to put them at their ease. '*The next person I will see is Muriel Thomas please*'.

The girl in the pink frock stood up. '*Come over here Miss Thomas and can I have your form please? Have you completed all these questions?*'

Muriel answered yes, and nearly curtseyed, she was so overawed by this sophisticated woman. Muriel thought although she was not young she looked like someone from a film she had recently seen.

'*I hope you have completed it correctly, we don't have any spare forms, paper is in short supply you know, there is a war on.*'

Muriel shyly approached Frances's desk and handed in the form. '*I am next. I was called up on the register. Here are the forms.*'

Frances looked her up and down. '*Thank you. Now, how old are you? You won't be enlisting yet, will you?*'

Muriel blushed at this estimation of her age and answered '*No, I am not old enough I am fifteen. My sister is in the ATS and my father isn't happy about her going away.*'

Frances thought for a moment while looking up and down the form, thinking she had neat handwriting, no mistakes. '*Then we may be able to employ you at the Ministry as a clerk. You will have to do this test.*' She handed her a form with questions typed neatly. '*How is your maths Muriel, you will need to be good at figures to work here?*' She didn't wait for an answer, but looked at her watch. '*Sit here please at this table. While you are doing that I'll see this young woman.*'

She saw the person who had sat next to her reading the newspaper while waiting. '*What is your name please?*' The other girl who looked somewhat older than Muriel answered, '*My name is Peggy Smith.*'

The Civil Servant asked her immediately, '*Peggy, are you a

local girl? You don't sound Welsh. Where are you from?' Since Peggy had only spoken her name she deduced that it was her appearance and fine clothing on which Miss Harrington had based her assumptions.

'*No Miss. I am from the Wirral.*' The tension made her speak quickly. '*We had to come here because our street was bombed. My family also lost their business, we had a printing firm. So we came here and we are in lodgings.*'

As the Civil Servant ushered Peggy into the room where Muriel was sitting at a table writing, Peggy noticed that Miss Harrington had a slight limp, and first wondered how she came by it, and then how she managed to walk in her high shoes. Had she had an injury, or was it the shoes, and vanity that caused the limp? Peggy was asked to sit down then Frances cordially remarked, '*I am so glad you were unhurt. Are you in good health now?*'

Peggy then looked down wondering if she should volunteer the information. But decided it was best to be truthful. '*No Miss, I have been in hospital, that's where I was when the street was bombed. And my family were visiting me – if they hadn't been – then we wouldn't be here now. I had my appendix out, so I was unable to join any of the forces as I wanted to do, they won't take any of us who have been in hospital.*'

Frances agreed, '*Yes, that's right, you have to be extremely fit because they would not want to have to pay out any early pensions. Well, what work **can** you do?*'

Now Peggy had further unfavourable news. '*I have never worked before and I am twenty eight.*'

Frances seemed exasperated. '*Well, where am I going to send **you**?*' Unbeknown to Frances a munitions factory had already turned Peggy down, even as a wages clerk, because of her inexperience. Neither could she assemble Jeeps. They had wanted shopgirls, those who were used to standing up on their feet all day. Some of the girls had learned to drive and were able to deliver the vehicles. (In fact Princess Elizabeth would learn to drive, but not until 1942.)

'But we **do** need thousands of clerks in all departments of the Ministry of Food. There are Food Offices all over Britain but this area is the headquarters for the whole country and there is so much work to be done.'

Now was the time for Peggy to disclose her secret ambition. 'I want to be a Civil Servant like you or...' she looked thoughtful... 'or I would like to work with the Queen's Messenger Convoys.'

Frances waited for a moment. She had to slot these people in where she could, and this girl Peggy was more mature than most, a city girl, and she was ambitious. What a pity she had no previous experience, neither had so many others. She felt sorry to hear her story that her family had come from the Wirral having lost everything. She empathised with Peggy over the bombing, she had had her own personal experience of that. It was not the shoes that had caused the limp. But as a professional she tried not to let her feelings affect her judgement. She would give Peggy the test, and perhaps she could have a fresh start, Frances was flattered that the young women saw her as a role model, and she seemed to know something about the Queens Messenger Convoys. Maybe she would make a career woman yet.

'Well we'll see what we can do Peggy, but as you have never worked before you may have to start at a very junior level like the other girls. Like this young lady Muriel here writing her test. Some employees will have to do some quite routine work all day like...like opening envelopes and salvaging them for re use. We have such a serious shortage of paper here. It's a boring job but someone has to do it.'

There had been collections of paper, for salvage, everything was reusable – even sadly diaries. There would have undoubtedly been some that would have been a valuable resource for historians one day, but so many were unfortunately lost. The memories would be mentally locked away with the older generation for posterity and if they did not relate those reminiscences then... gone. There was a letter in the local paper from the Librarian of the National Library of Wales appealing for secretaries of organisations to put aside papers with the intention of sending them to the National Library. They also advocated frugality with materials.

'The Ministry uses over 4000 tons of paper every year and one and a half million envelopes... if each employee saves one quarto sheet of paper per working day it will save 35 tons a year and these placed end to end would stretch from Rhos pier to the Dingle.'

Peggy was delighted that she would be able to work. She was determined she would not let Miss Harrington down, and would not waste any valuable paper by making any mistakes. She took off her leather gloves and set about filling in the form in her neat handwriting with her own fountain pen, which she had been given on her birthday.

Meanwhile, Frances Harrington cast a cursory glance over Muriel's test paper which she had been quietly but speedily completing. *'Mmm impressive, she has done this in record time, and her maths is certainly very good,'* thought Frances. *'Yes I could see that she would be very useful in the office of her friend Mr Elliot in "Butter and Cheese". Yes dear,'* she said to Muriel, *'Yes, you will do nicely. Now, tell me have you got a navy blue dress at home?'*

Frances quickly typed up a note, sealed it in an envelope – a reused one – and handed it to the girl, who smiled and said thank you, she knew she would enjoy working more than going to school.

Muriel smiled to herself as she glided down the steps outside the Metropole Hotel, she had been successful at the interview, her parents would be pleased with her. She clutched the letter given to her by Miss Harrington, in its slightly shabby recycled envelope and wondered about the contents. It was addressed to Mr Elliot at 'Butter and Cheese'. Although happy she also felt apprehensive, or even daunted by what she could expect at the office and hoped she could live up to expectations. Not long ago she was sitting at a school desk a little girl in a quiet seaside town, and suddenly she was a young woman approaching her first employment in a town which had been so suddenly invaded by sophisticated southerners, as well as the influx of evacuees and soldiers. Changes were happening so fast it made her head spin.

She arrived at the next hotel building, 'The Castle', where she had been told to look for Mr Elliot's department, and entered in with a mixture of elation and trepidation. As it was afternoon by now surely she wouldn't be expected to work today, although she really couldn't wait to start. No she assumed she was just introducing herself and arranging what time to go in the next day, finding out the rules and so on. And anyway she wasn't wearing her navy blue dress.

As she went up the steps through the swing door she saw a few other girls going about their business, they looked smartly dressed and well groomed, and were wearing lipstick. She did hope to get on well with them. She got directions from reception and found the door marked 'Mr J. Elliott' and knocked nervously. On hearing a voice from within say 'come in', she pushed the door into a room with two desks where two very different women sat in the anteroom to Mr Elliot's office.

On one side was a cheerful smiling middle-aged woman, wearing a suit with a pale blue blouse. Her hair was rolled into a sausage shape, which sat on top of her head sweeping back from above her brow, and when she turned her head Muriel could see other swirls coiled at the back. This would be the 'victory roll' she had heard of. Modelled on the manoeuvres of pilots but practical in getting long hair out of the way in industry.

'*Yes Miss, can we help you?*'

Muriel glanced at the other desk and saw a younger woman, not much older than herself, who didn't look happy at all. She had dark hair cut fairly short and waved around her square jaw. Her dark eyes blazed aggressively and her mouth turned down at the corners. *Whatever had upset her?* Muriel thought to herself. Since the less senior woman looked unapproachable, Muriel addressed the older woman handing her the envelope and saying, '*I have come from Miss Harrington's office, she says there is work here for me.*'

'*Yes that's right dear, we are expecting someone here to help out, we are just snowed under with work. Can you share Sadie's desk for now until we sort something out? Look, take that chair for a moment. Oh sorry, I am Mrs Humphries, by the way, and this is Sadie Kelly, who you will be working with. Would you mind starting this afternoon, you see we have a rush on and it's all got to be done? I'll give you some simple tasks because otherwise we will take all day explaining to you. Hang up your coat dear*'. She gestured to the bentwood coat stand, and then opened the envelope, carefully setting it aside for a further reuse, and read what Miss Harrington had written. Then smiling she seemed to change her mind saying, '*On second thoughts, can you check some accounts for me – I see you are good at maths.*'

Sadie was not pleased. She scowled and Muriel wasn't sure what she had done to upset her. There was obviously going to be a serious clash. Unbeknown to Muriel, Sadie had been inefficient. Miss Harrington had known about the situation in

Mr Elliot's office, the Elliots, John and his wife Marcia and their daughter Miranda, lodged at the same boarding house as Frances, and Frances had been looking out for a little gem like Muriel to send to rescue his department. Her maths test had been done in such record time and all quite correctly, so that Frances thought Muriel had been heaven sent for the job.

* * *

Muriel, having reminisced about the war days, was still sorting through her things. She had taken all her curios out of the china cabinet and lined up the silver on a table ready to polish. A black bin liner stood stiffly against the wall, she found it satisfying that she had steeled herself to dispose of so many old papers in one fell swoop. Documents that were well out of date. There were details of old insurance policies, both household and motor, gas bills, electricity, water rates, the lot so old it didn't warrant shredding, as well as old papers from her youth, almost overwhelming. Some she had put aside, all her families' collective memorabilia they would have to fetch and sort it themselves; it was not her responsibility to dispose of that. For herself, there were items such as her decades-old autograph book with entries by her former colleagues. She had been an administrator, and not just in this town, oh no she had been transferred to Guildford in the late 1940s. This had been a great adventure at the time, she would never have had an opportunity to move to the south without the Civil Service training she had received during wartime.

There was another reason why the move had been good for her, she and Herbert had got together during that move, fallen in love when they had both been transferred at the same time. She hadn't known him in Wales, but he had been so kind as to repair a puncture in her bicycle tyre outside the office in Guildford on their first meeting.

An old black and white photograph fluttered to the floor and she bent to retrieve it. A young man looked out proudly from the print. She quickly put it into the rubbish sack, she couldn't understand why she had kept that. She had had only one relationship before Herbert, and that had been disastrous. That young man in the photo was from the diamond tool factory, Benny. He had broken lot of hearts including Muriel's before he had run away with a girl who had briefly been a colleague of hers. The other girl had also worked at 'Butter and Cheese'. Muriel thought back to her first full day of employment in 1940.

* * *

That day Muriel had arrived at the office in the 'Castle Hotel' bright and early wearing her navy blue skirt, blue cardigan of her mother's and a white blouse crisply pressed. She had with her a sandwich for lunch, tomato with the minimal ration of ham which her mother had put by. She had almost skipped there she was so happy to be employed. She wondered what on earth she would have done after leaving school if the war had not come. Maybe she would have had to be a maid in one of the hotels.

She had tried to talk to Sadie in a friendly way at the end of the previous day and asked if she was walking the same way home as her, but the other girl was sullen and uncommunicative. Muriel had shrugged, not knowing what to make of her. The truth was Sadie felt her job was in jeopardy. She had made several mistakes, arrived late but had been kept on due to the volume of work that had to be got through. However, Mrs Humphries had realised that she was a spanner in the works, and that she was causing problems rather than alleviating work pressure. She just wasn't interested in making an effort, after all everyone had to pull together for the common good. There *was* a war on.

Mrs Humphries had hoped Sadie's call up papers were imminent, but no, Sadie was under age and would not be disappearing, for some time yet. While Muriel cheerfully and effortlessly went through columns and columns of figures Sadie was sent scowling to make tea. She took the caddy from the office shelf where it was kept and guarded safely and walked down the corridor to the hotel kitchen. But she had a plan which she formulated while she watched the kettle boil.

She had heard that the diamond factory had opened up in the top level of the hardware store on Princes Drive. Neighbours on Seaview Road had talked about it, The Wins family and Mrs and Mrs Frish had started the company 'Frish and Wins' on the third floor of the Bevans' building. It would have happened sooner, but the equipment coming from America had been torpedoed in Liverpool Bay and a second machine had had to be sent for.

There were to be different nationalities working there, Belgians like the Wins, and also French and Dutch machine operators. The Wins family were Jews who had escaped from their home in Antwerp in just the clothes they stood up in and with Gerrit Wins' briefcase containing rough diamonds he had saved from the clutches of the Nazis. The French police had given them safe passage to the coast and they climbed a rope ladder to board a ship arriving at Falmouth. After spending two months at a reception centre in the south, they heard from the older Wins boy Leo, who was by then stationed in Conwy, that the north Wales coast was a peaceful haven where you wouldn't even know there was a war going on. Peace was what Gerrit and

Frieda craved for themselves and their children, and that was how they came to arrive in the North Wales town. The site was also convenient for the port of Liverpool, to receive equipment and to ship consignments of navigational instruments for planes as part of the lend lease agreement with America.

Contemplating her career plan, Sadie sat on the draining board, swinging her legs, brooding and watching the steam rise, hatching her plan to escape from this boring stuffy office, working with these two women who she didn't particularly like, especially this new one, Muriel. Sadie was seething with jealousy not only of Muriel's looks but her numeracy skills, but she would show them, she would leave this office behind. Not caring whether butter and cheese would be distributed fairly through the country, she had a contact in a farm in the valley, she could get butter there, never mind what Lord Woolton said. And what of the rest of the country? Let Muriel and Mrs Humphries worry about that.

Sadie walked home that day to her boarding house via Seaview Road hoping to bump into Benny who often took that route between the Wins household and the factory on Princes Drive. She had met him at the Pier dance and had been to his boarding house to drink whisky in his room while his landlady wasn't looking, no 'ladies' were allowed in the bedrooms. What Sadie didn't know was that Mrs Parker, sleepless and anxious about the reputation of her establishment, had heard her leave in the early hours and standing in her curlers behind the curtains had watched Sadie as she made her way home by moonlight.

So Sadie's reputation was gone, not that she cared. Benny had cigarettes. Sadie fancied herself as a bit of a vamp after being mesmerised with the latest Hollywood movies on at the Odeon and the Arcadia, where she had learned to pout her scarlet lips as smoke curled from them. She had previously wanted to continue a relationship with a serviceman. To her chagrin, after a brief liaison he wasn't interested in her, and also what she didn't know was that that he had a wife at home already. That may not have prevented her from having her fun. Sadie was out to enjoy herself, thinking of the moment, because who knew what is in the future? There had been bombing in Manchester from whence she came. She stood in the shadows until Benny came around the corner. *'Hello there!'* she called to him seductively, standing with her hand on her hip, he stopped, looked over curiously and tempted, he sauntered in her direction. Now, she thought, she would put her plan into action.

Benny must have been some kind of foreman at the factory. He had some influence and was prepared to help Sadie. She had spun him some lies about why she had left her previous job, which wouldn't have washed with him, but that they happened to need someone to work in the office at the factory. Sadie was opportunistically in the right place at the right time. The next morning Muriel and Mrs Humphries had to make their own tea. Sadie did not show up for work.

CHAPTER 6

The schoolyard. County School. Wartime

At the secondary school the bell rang to signal the time for school morning break and there was a sound of desk lids slamming and children scrambling out into the playground shrieking excitedly and chattering as they went, in a variety of accents. A mix of northerners, southerners, and Welsh. Two of the older girls, newfound friends, walked over to a wall and sat down watching the younger children playing, running about mischievously, squabbling and laughing.

Since the weather had been kind, Miranda Elliot and her new friend sat on a wall basking in the sunshine. *'Oh thank heavens it's not raining like yesterday, I really hate it when the prefects make us stay outside even when it's wet.'*

This school was not quite what she was used to in Weybridge, but she had no choice but to attend since she had relocated with her family. Her father was a head of a department with the Ministry of Food. Miranda had missed all her own school friends, who had not been children of Civil Servants, and had been evacuated to other areas. Since arriving she had struck up a friendship with this local girl Mary Jones, who was a daughter of her landlady's friend. Mary, the same age as she, was as delightful a companion as she ever hoped to find in what she thought would be a remote corner on the coast of North Wales.

There had been some spats between the locals and the incoming influx; they all had to watch their step. Her parents had warned her, they all had to get on. Her father had important work to do, yet he had no choice but to relocate and was very glad to have a haven for his family away from the bombing. These were strange times, this town had suffered a huge upheaval, but think how bad it must be at home, never knowing when or where a bomb would fall.

Mary came from the very middle-class Jones family, genteel but not well to do. She was sometimes overawed by the sophistication of her new friend. She tried to keep Miranda's feet on the ground, helped her to settle in. One good friend had made all the difference to getting used to a new life a new environment. Mary now answered the comment about having to stay outside in the rain during break time: *'Well you wouldn't melt would you? You are sweet, ... but are you made of sugar?'* Miranda thought for a moment before responding thoughtfully, frowning and speculating that this girl knew very little about her. *'No I think I'm rather tough.'*

Mary thought again before speaking, wondering what had happened to Miranda before she arrived in the town. There had been an incident, she knew that much, but Miranda didn't want to talk about it to anyone. Mary hadn't wanted Miranda to think about those times, so had to divert her thoughts away from her friend's memories. So she continued, *'Yes you are right there, and you are clever. Yes you people from London get to learn Latin, and the ones from Manchester are doing French.'*

Miranda answered tactfully. She didn't want her friend to feel inadequate or deprived of learning the same subjects. *'Well you are doing Welsh,'* which was indeed a mystery to Miranda. Mary was very keen to learn Welsh. Although her mother was English her father was a welsh speaker. She knew it may not be of great use to her in the future, but the Welsh language had to be preserved for the future, and her grandparents spoke Welsh as a first language. There had been articles in the newspaper saying that the mass evacuation had had a diluting effect on the Welsh culture and language.

Mary and her father and so many others had been concerned about that when they read about it in the press. But this coastal town as it had burgeoned had after all not been predominantly Welsh from the start, a town which had grown with the advent of the railways, as had so many others in the nineteenth century. It developed with a mixed culture, having many connections with the nearby northern cities of Liverpool and Manchester. It was the towns to the west and the countrified areas, which had the overwhelmingly Welsh culture: '*I learn it only because my dad and I speak Welsh at home.*' Mary's father was from one of the inland towns.

'*And do you know what science I had to do?*'

No, Miranda didn't, and said so. Because they had the class split into groups it was extremely difficult for the teachers to plan, and to design a timetable with so many groups of children at different levels.

Mary wrinkled her nose and said in disgust, '**Domestic Science.** *Wearing a little white apron. Well we don't have much to cook do we? They just teach us how to do cleaning, how to wring out a dishcloth in a certain way... look you have to do it like this.*' She put her elegant pale hands out in front of her and mimed a demonstration.

Miranda thought how much Mary resembled a ballerina, graceful, slim and lithe, like the dancers she had seen when her parents had taken her to the *Nutcracker* in London before the war.

'*I expect they are training us for catering jobs for the town after* the war,' said Mary. 'That's not what I want to do, I always wanted to go to Ballet school in Chester if my parents will let me. But because of the war I may not be able to now.'

Miranda responded sensitively, and said in a soothing voice, 'Well it has changed a lot of things; I wanted to go to Art school in London.' Then suddenly that reminded her, she had a bit of news to tell. 'Did you hear Muriel has left school? She has got a job in the Civil Service! Said she was so unsure about her future it was for the best.'

Miranda looked interested, and commented, 'She was a very good student, top in our maths group. I am sure she will do well whatever she works at. If she is in the Ministry I will ask my Dad if she has joined his department.'

'Yes,' said Mary, 'But she wouldn't have left school to go into a catering job,' pensively returning to the issue of the catering training. 'I wonder if people will still want to come here for their holidays after the war.'

But Miranda exclaimed optimistically, 'But look, we wouldn't have met and become friends if it hadn't been for the war, and if my Dad hadn't been transferred from Whitehall to here.'

Both girls tried to count their blessings. 'Yes I am glad you came Miranda, you are safe here and I have learned a lot from you about other places. It was so quiet in this town before all of you came, the civil servants, the evacuees and the soldiers.' She thought she had learned more from conversations with Miranda than she had in class some days, the southern girl was very knowledgeable and spoke like an adult.

Mary continued: 'We are good friends aren't we? And when you go back after the war you will write to me won't you? Maybe come for a holiday?'

Miranda smiled enigmatically, wondering when and if the war would end. She had had a little first-hand experience, coming from the south, and she said graciously, *'Who knows how long that will be, but when the war ends yes of course I will. I am glad we came too. This is a lovely place to live and it's safer for us. But my Dad's job is important. He is not doing active service, his is a reserved occupation and I am sure what he is doing is really valuable. He met Lord Woolton the other day. It seems we may all be here for some time yet.'*

Mary was suitably impressed. *'Lord Woolton? Is he the one who wrote the recipe for the pie? It only has vegetables in it, not meat.'*

'Oh, I'm not sure if he wrote the recipe, I think it was a chef from the Savoy, but I know he recommends it,' said Miranda. He had in fact been photographed eating it for a press release, to encourage others.

'We have that on Tuesdays at our lodging, Mrs Owen makes it and she calls it "meatless Tuesdays".

'Well the pie was called after him. He is a good businessman, from Liverpool, not a politician, he gets on with the work, the Ministry headquarters are here, and the nation needs food. Our supplies are at such risk, being torpedoed. All these branches are here to see to it that everyone all over the country gets food, and that it is distributed fairly, and that people stick to the rules.'

Mary said, *'Yes, there are so many branches, the town has been quite taken over. It's funny to see all the different departments playing their sports teams against each other. "Bacon and Ham" beat "Animal feedstuffs" the other day in football. And then there was a team from all the Food Offices together playing against the Inland Revenue staff from Llandudno. We were all cheering "Go Food Go", it was so funny, and they won!'*

Miranda was smiling and animated, and had forgotten the sadness that had earlier preoccupied her thoughts. *'Yes and the Ministry staff join in with all the social activities too. My Mum is in the choir, she also works for the Ministry.'*

Mary was curious about Mrs Elliot. *'Your Mum! What does she do?*

Miranda proudly related, *'She is also a civil servant, and in the Queens Messenger Convoys. They organise the distribution of food all over the country to areas that have suffered disasters. She took up this work after...'* a shadow passed over her face as if there was something she wanted dismissed from her memory, *'...well, she has been doing it in the south too. She is also in the Home Guard.'*

Mary gazed, again impressed. *'I have seen your Mum, she is very smart. Her hair is beautiful and she wears nail polish.'*

Miranda not wanting to flaunt the glamour of her mother, since although sophisticated, she was actually quite a serious person, said quietly, *'If she has any left.'*

But Mary went on with the comparison between their two mothers, saying, *'My Mum wears an apron all day and stays at home cleaning. When does your Mum find time to do her housework and look so glamorous?'*

'Don't forget, we are in rooms,' said Miranda, *'so our landlady cooks for us. We couldn't find a property to rent. The newspaper is full of people advertising that they need a house to rent. We have to live where we can. But I would rather be here than in the south at this time'.*

Mary countered: *'We have evacuees at my house, they came from Liverpool. It's awfully crowded. Do you know what the little boy said to my mum the other day?*

Miranda looked amused and had to as, *'What did he say?'*

'He said, "Missus Jones, why do you never sit on the doorstep, like my mother?"'

Even more fascinated now Miranda was incredulous and asked Mary, *'Do they do that in Liverpool? They don't do it where I come from either, they wouldn't think of it!'*

'It seems that's what they do in Scotland Road,' said Mary, *'But

maybe it's a good idea as there is hardly anywhere else to sit at the moment. And another thing, do you know the children didn't know milk came from a cow, they thought it came from a bottle?'

Miranda laughed, then thought and said, 'I see the mothers breastfeeding their babies out in the street. I never saw that before, not in Weybridge'

'No', said Mary, 'We never saw that here either before the war. With all these people coming into the town, it has opened eyes. We knew nothing about people from other towns before the war. I have been to Liverpool with my parents on the train, but only to the big shops. Well we knew nothing about what sort of people live there.'

The bell rang for the start of the next lessons and they had to hurry to fetch their books. Miranda had to go to a Latin class and Mary to learn Welsh. But Miranda had a parting question for Mary, something to think about before they met up at lunchtime. 'Mary, Shall we go to the dance at the pier pavilion on Saturday?'

Now Mary was incredulous, and thought how daring her friend was. 'Oooh I don't know if my dad will let me. There will be a lot of soldiers there.'

But Miranda was not deterred, her answer was, 'I think I will only be allowed to dance with the telegraph students from the wireless college, they are boys of about our age. Mary, you can help me practice the steps.'

Mary thought about it again, why not after all. 'We mustn't stay out too late then.'

'It will cost two and six,' said Miranda, 'And we can only drink water.'

Mary said, 'Well we are only sixteen and still at school.'

Both giggled and hurried off to their lessons looking forward to their plan.

CHAPTER 7

Stargazing

The Prom

It was two weeks after Miranda and Mary had carried out their daring plan to go to a dance at the Pier. They had enjoyed the adventure, feeling very grown up. Neither the Elliots or the Jones parents were very keen on the idea, but came round to it, it was all part of growing up, their two daughters behaved very responsibly. The Elliots were glad that Miranda had settled in the town and they wanted to encourage the friendship she had struck up with the local girl, Mary, although they thought her rather young for her age.

The two girls decided that the on following weekend they would meet on Friday evening at the 'Princess' cinema, opposite the Metropole buildings. They wanted to see '*Gone with the Wind*' with Clarke Gable and Vivienne Leigh. At the cinema the strains of music accompanying the Pathe newsreel could be heard in the background. They bought their tickets and waited excitedly in the entrance for a short while since they had arrived separately and wanted to chat.

Miranda had dressed casually, but in clothes that looked as if they were expensive. Mary looked beautiful in her outfit and her pale blonde glossy shoulder length hair was curled under and rested on her collar. Miranda was surprised at the difference in her friend's appearance; Mary seemed to have grown up overnight.

'*Mary where did you get that dress?*' She knew the family struggled financially, and were not as well off as her own.

'*It's my cousin's we altered it. She has outgrown it now. Does it look alright?*' She twirled gracefully while Miranda clasped her hands in delight, genuinely pleased for her friend.

'*Oh you did a good job. You look much older than sixteen. It must be the pink lipstick.*'

Mary took a small package out of her bag. '*Yes, the colour is called "Shimmering heartbreak pink"; look it came wrapped just in paper, as there's no metal available to make the cases during the war. I got that from my cousin too*'.

'*Mary, take these sweets and put them in your bag,*' said Miranda. She had asked her mum to get them with the last of the coupons they had.

Mary hurriedly put them away as well as the lipstick, had become distracted by something much more interesting to them both. '*Oh look, there's that young man from the information bureau who we met at the pier dance last week. You know the one who has gone to work for the Ministry now. Shall we ask him to sit near us?*'

Miranda glanced over his way casually, and spotted him. '*Yes, I know him, he works at my Dad's office now, he was in billeting, but he has transferred. Shouldn't we wait for him to ask us?*'

Mary became flustered. '*He's coming over.*'

The chap approached them confidently and spoke. '*Hello Miranda. Your father said you would be here tonight.*'

'*Yes,*' she said,'*he agreed to me coming. Do you know Mary?*' said Miranda. The young man looked over and said, '*Oh yes, we danced at the pier last week. Mary, you are a very good dancer.*'

'*Hello Alf,*' said Mary. '*Thank you. I have recently heard that I have a place at the Chester ballet school next term.*'

'Oh well done. Yes you told me you had applied. Is it all right for me to join you ladies?' said Alf.

Mary looked down shyly, but said, 'Yes Alf. But the music is now playing, I think we should go in or we will miss the start of the film.'

The music played the MGM theme, and the three of them walked towards their seats. They had been so looking forward to 'Gone with the Wind'. Mary offered some of the sweets Miranda had given her and which she was keeping in her handbag. It had been kind of Miranda, she must have used all the points she had left in her ration book for them.

'Alf would you like one of these?'

'Oh thank you,' he said rustling his sweet wrapper. Then before savouring the sweet he plucked up the courage to ask, 'Mary, would you like to go to the dance at the Pier tomorrow?'

She was overjoyed. She liked him very much and said, 'Oh yes Alf, but can Miranda come too?'

'I should think so,' said Alf, then he seemed pensive while chewing on the sweet.

Miranda looked over at him asking, 'Are you alright Alf?'

The music of the film played dramatically in the background, but he looked preoccupied and said, 'Mary? What sort of sweet is this?'

'Humbug I think, Alf.' She thought he seemed distracted, but put it down to his concentration on the film.

* * *

Several weeks later on Colwyn Bay Promenade Mary and Alf sat in one of the shelters, cosily wrapped together. Although their relationship was short they knew their true feelings for each other. They had walked along the sand, hand in hand, beside the incoming tide, beachcombing until the moon shone, and had collected some pretty white cockle shells and white stones washed smooth by rough tides.

'*Darling what a beautiful night it is,*' Alf said to her.

Mary seemed to have grown up fast in the last few weeks. She was seventeen by now and had left school. '*I agree, you wouldn't think there is a war on.*'

Alf continued: '*It's so quiet and peaceful here on the prom looking out across the sea. I wonder what is happening in Liverpool, it is so near to us. Friends who have arrived here in the past week say the bombings have caused an awful lot of damage with people now homeless. There are a lot of evacuees still here, what a problem it is to get people to take in young children into their homes. So many of the women work now, as clerks for the ministry or munitions or assembling those jeeps I saw all parked on the road. They were on Gregory Avenue.*'

Mary said, '*This morning when I looked out of my window the sky over there was red with the sunrise.*'

'Oh dear,' said Alf, then, '"*Shepherd's warning*" – *not good weather to come.*'

The sound of a German bomber was suddenly heard overhead, and Alf said, '*What can I hear? Gerry is on his way – we are right under the flight path and it won't be long before we are seeing anti-aircraft fire and then the flames rising up over there – it was awful watching it a few nights ago and there is nothing we can do about it. They say that Gerry is using the lights of Dublin to get a bearing on Liverpool.*'

'*Alf,*' said Mary, '*I shall be so worried about you when you go away to be a telegraphist. I will be in Chester then. Do you think I should not go after all. No one expected the war to go on this long, but should I go and train for some kind of war work instead?*'

Alf hugged her tight and kissed her forehead. She was so

sweet. *'No darling, ballet has always been your dream, and you are so young still. Look if the war is still on after you have trained, then perhaps you can work for the ministry later on. But the war will end soon, you'll see.'*

Mary smiled up at him, saying, *'Really darling? If you think it's alright, then I'll go. I am going to miss you so much when you are away, the dancing will be a diversion for me.'*

At the mention of dancing he could not resist, but sprang up on to his feet and whisked her in circles. They danced on the promenade oblivious to all around them. The waves crashed and lapped up the jetty near to where they stood, and she giggled overjoyed and not caring that their feet got wet. The moon shone and there were stars in their eyes, in those carefree days of not knowing what lay ahead.

CHAPTER 8

The past is revealed

The Jones' house

Mary and Miranda were at the Jones's household that evening doing some maths and English homework together, as well as watching over and entertaining the children. Jenny Jones had gone out to visit Olwen so the girls had the responsibility of looking after the evacuees. The two girls had taken a kindly interest in the young ones and as a diversion for them both. Mary had coached Rita in some dance steps, both teacher and pupil had been delighted by it, and the young flame-haired girl had taken to it like a natural performer.

Mary found she had a natural talent for teaching. Rita also was in good singing voice. It had been planned that Mary would take part in the Ministry concert in the ballroom of the Castle Hotel and she wanted to include little Rita in some of the dance routines. Miranda, however was not keen to go to the theatrical performance, although she joined in with activities in the house.

'It's going to be in the ballroom of a hotel, not the theatre,' soothed Mary, unable to understand the aversion Miranda had for theatrical performance when she had been happy to go to the cinema. The 'Castle' was one of the many hotels requisitioned by the Ministry for their offices, but it happened to have a very good ballroom which was ideal for small concerts given by the staff. In addition there was Penrhos College, the huge club where thousands of Ministry staff socialised, and of course the Pier pavilion, that would be for really big concerts, and Mary had been asked to join in their pantomime 'Babes in the Wood'. Many of the civil servants played musical instruments and they were surely not going to give up their orchestra just because their department had been evacuated. Ministry folk brought a great deal of culture into the area and they meant it to continue that way. As well as plays at the theatre there were art classes. They entertained themselves very well. Mary had asked her mother to make some sort of costume for Rita, Jenny was very good with a needle, they wanted to look in the Owen's loft to see what they could convert. Jenny was good at recycling all sorts of garments, but before Mary could broach the subject there was a huge disruption.

Out of the blue there was a loud crash and the two girls looked out of the window. They saw black smoke pouring in clouds up into the sky in the direction over the Owens's guesthouse and Miranda started to panic.

'Breathe deeply,' said Mary, trying to keep calm although worried at how her friend had reacted, 'here's a paper bag, breathe into this, it will be alright' and then... 'but I want this bag back afterwards.'

This made Miranda laugh and brought her back from wherever she had been momentarily. Mary had thought it must have been a dark place, but tactfully didn't press her for answers. 'Let's go and see, Norah next door will have the children for us.'

They put on their shoes and coats and scrambled out, planning to first deposit Jimmy and Rita with Norah (under protest) and then to investigate the damage. Miranda was visibly still shaking. Mary knew that she had had a bad experience in the past but had never dared to ask about it. She had at first been more concerned about the children, that they might be frightened, but they hadn't realised it might be serious. '*But Miranda, this is a safe area, so you don't need to worry,*' she tried to reassure her, although no one really knew how safe they were, or how long the war would continue and what the outcome would be.

'*I know Mary, but I have to go and see if everything is alright. I just have to.*' Now she was close to tears and fighting them back.

'*Yes we will then, but please don't be so upset, look you are shaking, and I don't want the children to see,*' said Mary.

They quickly took Rita and Jimmy round to the neighbour Norah, who had been alarmed to hear the noise too, but didn't mind at all having the children, and they explained to her that they would be very careful and that they needed to reassure Miranda. Then they stumbled down the road to see what the disturbance was.

Mary was very apprehensive, more because of her friend's reaction than what she expected to find. Of course she had no experience of any attack or casualties in the area, she was oblivious of what the consequences might be.

For Miranda it was a different story. They arrived panting to the Owen household and were relieved to find all was well. Smoke was still rising beyond the buildings in the next street where there had been a house fire, the cause of which was unknown. The crowd in the street were busy speculating. 'It was a log fallen out of the grate, caught fire on the rug.' 'People should be more careful.' Some had other explanations. 'That's not what I heard, no it was the stove that was faulty'. Whatever the cause the spreading flames had engulfed the kitchen and combustible material elsewhere in the house had caused a small explosion.

The residents and neighbours had acted quickly and

although blackened, the house was still just about habitable, it had to be, there was no other option for the women of the household who were wringing their hands in despair and crying on the street.

'*We had little enough and now this, how are we going to cope?*' one woman wailed, wiping her face on her apron. Black streaks of soot were mixed with tears. They were mortified by the damage, but they were also suffering from shock having first thought that this was an attack.

'*There there, Agnes, I know you've had a great shock but think on, no one is injured. Come home with me luv, I'll get the kettle on and you can have a wash at my place. The men are locking up now, you can all stay at mine tonight, your two evacuees an all, we'll manage somehow.*' Two bedraggled children stood with a blanket round their shoulders.

Miranda although full of compassion for this household was beside herself with relief that it had been just a minor incident with no one hurt. It was caused by carelessness not by the war and Mary thought the overreaction slightly odd, and said so. Maybe this was the time to talk about the past. '*See, your family are safe, it wasn't your boarding house now, so no need to worry. Your parents will be safe at the Owen's. And I'll walk back there with you.*'

Miranda looked into her friend's eyes and with steely determination said, '*Well alright then, I owe you an explanation. I'll tell you what happened to us. But let's go somewhere quiet.*'

They walked over to the Owens' garden and sat outside on the garden bench overlooking the vegetable plot, where they could talk privately. They sat quite still next to the peas and beans growing on strings attached to poles, hoping to have a little privacy there.

A soldier came out of the house and lit up a cigarette, but

kept his distance and they were sure he would not overhear them. Everyone's houses were so crowded these days.

'*Poor Agnes, and those little children,*' said Mary.

Miranda started to speak with an unusually faltering tone, unlike her confident self. '*Now I'll tell you what happened to us. Before we were evacuated here with my father's work, we used to go to the theatre often in London. On this particular night I went with my mother and a friend, Emily. We often used to go as a treat, and where we lived is not far on the train from central London. At the start of the war the theatres and cinemas had closed immediately,*'

'*Yes, here too,*' said Mary at this gap in conversation. '*I suppose they were regarded as a target for large gatherings at first when war broke out.*'

Miranda nodded and went on. '*Yes, but they opened again when the bombing did not accelerate as it was first thought it might, and you know, it's so good for morale to have entertainment.*'

Mary was pleased to hear this said. It gave her some credit for the roles she played in the local theatre, and strengthened her ambition to be a professional dancer. She leaned in to Miranda, who was about to confide something to her.

'*We had been in the stalls enjoying the performance, it was a musical, and were startled to see that the stage set was vibrating, wobbling and collapsing, the actors were running off in all directions. We looked at each other and thought, this could not be a part of the performance.*'

Then without warning they heard a terrible crash, – deafening it was, and they were terrified, clinging on to each other not knowing what to do in the dark. As their eyes grew accustomed to the dark they saw that the set on stage was completely smashed, the footlights had blown, exploded , so that that too was in darkness. Pieces of masonry were falling around them and there was an acrid smell of burning. The tier above them was collapsing and they found themselves thrown to the floor. They were so lucky to have been sitting in the stalls near the front and not under the balcony.

Emily was lying next to Miranda under a seat and she was very still. Her mother got up and tried to help the girls to their feet so that they could escape out on to the street. The roof had come off making the stars visible and they could see an opening where the outside wall was torn apart, Miranda's mother was trying to get them out that way, to the street but they couldn't get Emily up.

Miranda paused here and shuddered. *'Oh I'm so sorry Miranda, I didn't realise, I shouldn't have asked.'*

Mary gently said, taking her arm. *'No, its alright. She wasn't dead. I can talk about it now. At first I had nightmares all the time, in fact, I lived those moments over and over, like flashbacks – even when I was awake. You see that's why I never talked to anyone about it before'.*

She went on: *'I realized then that Emily was unconscious, and people were telling me to more along there but mother and I couldn't think of leaving her where she lay, but... you are not supposed to move an injured person. She remained under the seat, my mother and I managed to drag it off her. She had been trapped by her legs, and there was blood covering her body. My first thought was, that's her new dress, what will her mother say when she gets home... how silly of me.*

I didn't realize just how badly she was hurt. I had been lucky, I was conscious, but very dazed, and aware of a large gash on my leg from a piece of masonry that had fallen off the ceiling. It seemed to be the biggest cut, and blood was spurting out. Mother told me squeeze with my hands to try and close the wound, I wrapped my silk scarf around it while she looked after Emily holding her hand and telling her that everything was alright. Mother called out to a man to help her, and they managed to bring Emily round. We didn't know if the whole building was going to collapse, so we had to all get out of there quickly. There was so much noise of people screaming in terror. I was just frozen... And then someone came to help. I managed to get up in the darkness, I could walk but I couldn't see where I was going, and stumbling over all the rubble. It seemed ages before two men came with a little lamp and they helped me out in the darkness. Emily was laid on a stretcher and they carried her out of the gap where the wall had been. Mother and I followed on to the hospital to be with her.'

'Oh, Miranda. *Was she alright?*' Mary was appalled by what she was hearing.

'*Well yes she lived, but she had to walk with crutches, she still does, and will do for a long time... maybe all her life. She doesn't remember much about it as she passed out again and awoke in the hospital. She had concussion too. Her parents are not civil servants, so they had no postings planned, but after this they took her away to her grandmother in the country. I hope to see her again after the war. But there were others there that night who did not survive the blast. They died, and I can't stop thinking about it.*'

The two sat in silence contemplating what had been said and Mary found it difficult to know how to respond, so she just held Miranda's hand while she continued the story.

'*I can never forget the terrible shock and fear. The smell of burning and smoke was awful and it remains with me whenever I think about that day. Having got me and Emily out my mother went back inside to see if she could be of further help to the rescue teams, people were telling her not to, to go back outside, but she said she couldn't help herself, and nobody could stop her, they were too busy anyway and I was beside myself waiting until I saw her come out helping a lady who was limping and coughing from the smoke. It was thought that there were other high explosive bombs which had either failed to explode or they were fitted with delayed-action fuses, and one unexploded device was being worked upon by bomb disposal experts.*

Mother was so calm and brave. Despite the chaos, when reassured the rest of the audience from the unaffected areas of the theatre reacted calmly and as directed by the stage manager on a megaphone they made their way out.'

For a moment Miranda put her hand on her mouth and laughed. Mary was shocked at this, but this was what was known as 'gallows laughter', with the shock of the terrifying memory.

Miranda continued. *'As we left there was one of the band members still in the orchestra pit. His evening suit was in tatters, and he was soaked with the water from the fireman's hose. His face was black with soot, and do you know he was still playing his instrument... what tune was that he played now? "There'll always be an England" wasn't it? Of course although he was not injured, miraculously, he was in deep shock too. As we waited on the pavement for the makeshift ambulance... it was just a van... I noticed that the roadside was sparkling with frost and glittering broken glass from the windows on the street, we stepped over some of the merchandise from the shops which had their goods scattered on the pavement, no one took any notice of them, they were untouched. Then when we got to the hospital we had to telephone Emily's parents to tell them what had happened. We were so afraid for her.'*

'Then what about your leg?' asked Mary.

'Oh, that's alright. I have a scar,' Miranda dismissed it. *'But Mother and I were so lucky to have escaped with just cuts and bruises.'* But Miranda, and others had deep mental scars: *'And of course we were so shaken, and we didn't know what had happened anywhere else, whether our own house was still standing. I tell you, we felt so lucky to be transferred to this town. But we were very traumatised – you see, that's why I could never talk about it until now, and even when I look across at Liverpool and imagine what is going on there.*

'Before we came here we had to spend a few nights in our Anderson shelter at the bottom of the garden, and when we came out

of it each morning not knowing what we would find when we emerged. People were killed in their shelters you know... they are not reliable.'

At this Mary look utterly horrified and, speechless, covered her mouth with her hands.

'I'll tell you something else,' said Miranda.

'What?' said Mary.

'Miss Harrington, she is my father's colleague, she works in personnel, you know she lives here at our boarding house too. She was there that night. Have you seen her limping?'

'Yes I had noticed', said Mary.

'And what about Rita's mother in Liverpool?' added Mary, 'do you know when she came to visit she insisted on taking little Billy back with her to Liverpool! I know he has missed her, but how could she be so selfish?'

* * *

In what had been a terraced street in Liverpool a small boy opened his eyes shocked to find himself in the smouldering wreckage of his former home. It was dark as pitch, and dusty. He had been hiding under the stairs while the air raid siren wailed. Coughing up dust he wiped the tears with his hand, whimpering softly. There was no one to hear him, he was not badly hurt but still very shaken. He didn't know where his Mammy was, when the siren started he had immediately run into the under stairs cupboard, too frightened to go out alone to the air raid shelter. The cupboard door was splintered and hanging off its hinges.

If he just waited here quietly perhaps she would come and get him, he had no idea how long he had been asleep since that bump on the head. He knew she would come for him, she must be hiding somewhere herself. He so wished his brother and sister were here, they would know what to do, they always looked after him. The oversized pyjamas he was wearing had been brought back with him from Wales, hand-me-downs from the WVS collection. They were so uncomfortable now, they were wet and cold.

Rubbing the bruise on the back of his head caused by some falling plaster, he saw all around him that pieces of masonry were still dropping at random. A shaft of light had entered since the last shift and he looked around at the bricks and fallen debris strewn around. He picked one half brick up with two hands; they were really heavy he thought, not like the wooden ones in the little truck Uncle Emlyn had given him. He remembered that during the carefree days when he had built towers of brightly painted wooden bricks they had eventually collapsed.

He sat rocking back and forth quietly humming to himself. Instinctively he knew he had to get out of here, he could smell smoke and was very afraid, where was his Mammy? Would anyone come for him? Maybe not. Tentatively he felt his way in the darkness, his little hands looking for spaces to crawl through, he knew he was just small enough to get through certain gaps in the debris. He tried to push aside a loose joist, but it was too heavy for him, then there was a creaking sound and another loud crash, he screamed in terror then all was quiet, he could no longer speak.

Beyond the site of his fear there were acres more devastation, survivors and many beside themselves looking for their lost loved ones.

CHAPTER 9

Concert

At the 'Castle Hotel'

Jenny Jones had been horrified when she returned home to find that that her daughter and her friend had gone out to see what the commotion was on the night of the explosion, especially as the girls had not returned immediately. Mary had said they were talking in the Owen's garden, on the bench beside the vegetable patch, but she didn't say what they had talked about. The incident had not been forgotten but had served to remind them all what a comparatively safe place they lived in, and were grateful for that, especially survivors of other incidents.

Jenny herself had heard the blast from Olwen's loft while they were searching among the old finery in a trunk belonging to Olwen's late grandmother. Old Mrs Weynton had been well to do and fond of foreign travel. As a young woman she had been on 'the grand tour of Europe' as was customary for young ladies of affluent families. They would have needed to do it in style, and this was evident by the wardrobe she had saved packed up in a trunk and various hatboxes for posterity. The clothes had been inherited by Olwen as the only granddaughter. The two women had been enjoying themselves searching through, amused at the old styles, yet grateful that Olwen had kept these items, because the fabric was of superior quality, had been well preserved in naphthalene and all would surely come in handy now. Olwen had already *made over* several garments for her own family as recommended in the 'Make do and mend' posters published by the government, who wanted people to go on wearing their own old clothes.

Olwen had made over all the most practical garments with wools tweeds and cottons and what was left was not practical for everyday wear. There was a silk kimono with rich embroidery, ruched sleeping caps, lace edged, petticoats, peignoirs and ball gowns. The grandmother had even kept her wedding dress and veil. The stench of mothballs was not unbearable, but they had at least been effective, all fabrics were in good order and everything had been sealed away for decades. Then they found what they were looking for. Inspiration! A pale pink satin evening gown and some marabou trim was discovered. Jenny had visions of transforming it into a ballet outfit for Rita, and lucky that she was such a little thing, then there would be enough material, and some left over perhaps for a little cape. Her bright auburn curly hair would look stunning against the baby pink satin, thought Jenny, and a discarded outgrown pair of ballet pumps came in handy.

Jenny sat and sewed by hand in the evening listening to the radio and thinking. There was a secret radio station which William Joyce (or Lord Haw Haw as he was known) used to broadcast. It terrified her when she heard him say *'Germany calling, Germany calling... We know where you are Ministry of Food';* because she wondered if the town would be bombed. Chills went down her spine. All those who heard it were terrified. Not only that, there would have been chaos if the administration of the food supplies for the whole country were disrupted.

There had been thought to be Celtic Nationalism used to recruit Nationalist spies. In 1941 Lady Rhys Williams had said that she had been canvassed as a possible fifth columnist by the wife of the successor of Ribbentrop, who sought an admission that Wales was seething with disaffection. However Lady Williams impressed upon her that there was no more loyal a people. Only two Nazi collaborators were identified in the area in those days, but 156 suspects were under MI5 secret surveillance. William Joyce, the infamous Irish propagandist, had arrived as a friend and sub-tenant of Philby, father of Kim in 1937. The evacuated variety department of the BBC in Bangor and Llandudno responded to Joyce's broadcasts, by trying to schedule the most popular entertainment simultaneously.

Jenny had only two evacuees to look after now since Mrs Gerard had come from Liverpool and taken young Billy home with her. The family tried to persuade her not to, pleaded with her, but the little boy had missed her even though his brother Jimmy and sister Rita had done their best to comfort him. All the evacuee children had missed their homes and parents, many had been given new insights and experiences. Billy had been well off where he was, within the Jones family house was an atmosphere of overwhelming and welcoming kindness.

Now in preparation for the imminent concert Jenny was happy to create this costume for Rita, along with her daughter Mary and other performers. This was her contribution, it cost nothing, and the creativity was recreational and therapeutic to her now that she had some time to herself. Jimmy had gone fishing with Emlyn on the pier. The tide was coming in, they wouldn't need to go to the end, and they couldn't. Planks had been removed in case of invasion. People thought this rather strange since the tide would never be high enough for any boat to dock. Jenny hoped to have mackerel again for supper and if the boys came back with it, they would invite their neighbour Norah to join them. She was an elderly widow. Rita loved to sit with her and hear stories going back to Victorian times, Rita was there now lying on her stomach on a rag rug in front of the hearth with her chin propped on her elbows at old Mrs Griffiths' feet, looking up in wonder and taking it all in, and the old lady liked nothing better than to sit with her tabby cat purring on her lap in front of the fire and have an audience eager for her tales. Rita would remember them all her life and relate them to her own family. Her favourites were about the Rose Queen... or the time a plane arrived on the local golf course... then there was Prince Madoc who sailed from the local harbour to discover America before Columbus. Meanwhile next door, Jenny smiled to herself as she completed the costume to her own design. She had innate artistic talent. She made the piping to form appliqué with her nimble fingers and covered the buttons on the satin dress. It was a pleasure to do this for Rita and she knew how much she would appreciate it. She imagined how when Rita saw it she would glow with delight. Maybe there would be a write up about the concert in the local paper again.

'The Ministry of Food staff recently demonstrated their talents in the realm of music by giving excellent performances of The Messiah last week members of the dramatic society showed their capabilities once more proving that the Ministry is rich in amateur talent. The ambitious programme at the Colwyn Bay Pier Pavilion included four one act plays.'

* * *

By March 1941 productions of Du Maurier's *Rebecca* and J. B. Priestley's *When we are Married* were staged at the Repertory Theatre, and in April the Music Society gave a concert to a packed audience in the Penrhos assembly hall, the orchestra comprising mainly of Ministry of Food personnel. The local paper had reported: *'Although the orchestra of thirty eight was augmented by a small number of professional players the majority were members of the Ministry of Food which is fortunate to possess this wealth of talent. The choir consisting entirely of members of the Ministry, numbered nearly one hundred.'*

On the day of the concert Rita was ecstatic to be wearing such a beautiful dress, Jenny really was very talented, and imaginative as well as practical. Mary had inherited her mother's artistic flair, but in another direction, in dance, and had put all her efforts into teaching the younger evacuee girl. She was rewarded with a faultless performance, and the discovery that a future in teaching could be hers, perhaps after the war. *'Goodness,'* thought Mary, *'she is already as good a dancer as me, after all the training I have had, and she is also a very good singer.'* But only the dancing was a credit to her teaching skills. Rita had perfect pitch and was gifted with an extraordinary voice.

At the interval refreshments were given in a collection of assorted cups and glasses. Contributions had been brought by everyone, it would otherwise have been impossible to arrange. What little they shared was wholeheartedly appreciated and the ambiance was one of warmth and friendship. Muriel carried a tray of tea carefully, stopping at intervals as people stopped her to chat to en route, it was unlikely that she would get the tea there before it was stone cold at this rate. In this small town networking was natural. She had friends within the staff and fitted in well into her new role as accounts clerk, making it a point to get along with everyone. She had heard unfavourable reports about her predecessor, not that the staff were prone to gossip, they were far too busy for that, at least during working hours, although after work was a different matter. They looked on it as showing concern and interest in others. Muriel had heard that Sadie had found employment in the diamond factory, and had a boyfriend there too. Well, as long as she was happy there, as she wasn't missed at her previous position.

She had just collected the last cup when Mrs Humphries stood up at the front of the ballroom with an announcement. Her teaspoon chimed on a glass and her voice rang out: *'We are so happy to welcome you here to the Castle Hotel Ballroom tonight, at this concert organised by "Butter and Cheese" as this is the venue of those very offices. We are grateful for the help of "Animal feedstuffs department" for their contribution in organising the collections for the refreshments. As many of you know this is a concert run by the Ministry, but we could not have managed without the support and generous offers of help from the local community. In particular I would like to thank Mary Jones for her choreography of all the other dancers taking part, as well as thanking her for her own wonderful performances. Also we are very grateful to Mary's mother Jenny Jones for the costumes she and Mrs Olwen Owen have provided for some of you tonight. Here she is.'* And Mrs Humphries gestured over to where Jenny was shyly sitting.

To Jenny's embarrassment everyone looked at her and clapped. *'Also, thank you to Muriel Thomas for organising the refreshments. We will be having a small collection for the spitfire fund and I ask you, if at all possible to donate what you can afford... We hear that the spitfire is going to be called "Colwyn Bay", so we are very keen to get it airborne as soon as possible... The next concert will be held at the Pier ballroom, since we have had such a good turnout here tonight we really do need bigger facilities...'*

Rita, peeking out from behind a velvet curtain was a little nervous, waiting in the wings for her turn. She watched wide-eyed as many others performed before her, and absorbed everything going on around her. Mary had danced classical ballet beautifully and Rita was in awe of her, then many others had recited, played instruments and sung in turn, some were locals, others displayed the skills they had brought from London or Manchester.

There had been a scary moment when one of the Ministry women had sung a song which had always belonged in the repertoire of a particular local woman, Beth, who was consequently not impressed. She sat grim faced with her arms folded and her mouth clamped in a hard line, and glaring, racking her brains thinking of what she could sing instead when it was her turn. The younger children sitting crossed legged on the front row could hear the comments whispered around them and took all this in, giggling behind their hands.

There was a wide cross section of employees from so many different departments of the Ministry, and others besides, the ballroom was crowded to bursting point with many small children allowed to be up late, to come and sit on the floor, or on their parents' laps. Rita could see Jimmy sitting with Jenny, he was cross legged at her feet with his face scrubbed and his hair combed and parted at the side, and slicked down with water. He claimed he preferred football and fishing, and he had lately missed the companionship of his brother in these, however it would be a night he would remember all his life as he had never seen anything like it, and he was suitably impressed.

A treat was in store for him, wait till he saw his sister singing and dancing in front of the crowd, he nearly burst with pride. He was to remember this for the rest of his life and relate the story down the generations.

Finally it was her moment, and with racing heart Rita took to the stage like a natural performer. The musicians struck up the Delibes ballet tune and Rita lost in a world of music that would become her life. She came to life like the doll in the story of the ballet 'Coppelia' and people watched enraptured at how one so young, just eleven years old, could give such an excellent performance with comparatively little training or guidance. She snatched up a mirror and a powder puff, props from a small table and used them to mime to the dance. The tempo quickened and at one stage in a later dance she threw tiny party favours wrapped in tissue, whirling, mesmerising the crowd, parcels landed; a home-made bon bon here, a hair ribbon to a little girl, a tiny bell... trinkets passed on, of no value except for the magic it bestowed on the catchers of these 'treasures.'

But the most valuable aspect was the experience, the spectacle, and the room was silently spellbound in wonder. Rita sang songs she had learned, popular songs of the day, but at the rendition of *'Home sweet home'* there was not a dry eye in the house. Rita maintained composure, no one in the room knew what was to be in the future for any of them, but one thing Rita knew was that she wanted passionately to go on to be a performer. She adored Mary and wanted to be like her. Rita was a star in the making. She had one more dance and song to perform, which would steal the show.

A tall teenage boy leaned against the wall watching. He had left his fellow scouts on the journey home and slunk in unnoticed to watch the performance. A son of one of the Jewish diamond workers, he did not usually mix with these amateur theatrical people, he had no talents for performing but was an appreciative spectator. He silently watched the young girl a few years his junior, shyly wishing he had an introduction to this circle.

Rita's last dance was based on the story of 'The Nightingale' which was a literary fairy tale by Danish poet and author Hans Christian Andersen about an emperor who prefers the tinkling of a bejewelled mechanical bird to the song of a real nightingale.

When the Emperor is near death, the nightingale's song restores his health. The tale is believed to have been inspired by the author's unrequited love for opera singer, Jenny Lind. The story has been adapted to opera, and ballet. Rita was able to dance and also sing to this theme.

Mary watched her protégé proudly. This was all her doing, the choreography of the dance, teaching the steps and the theme. She felt some empathy for young Rita, having herself been obsessed having danced from a young age. But she could not take any credit for Rita's extraordinary voice. Now Mary was becoming equally enthusiastic about the innate teaching skills she had discovered in herself.

She and Miranda had been sitting next to Miss Harrington for the performance. Mary had noticed with admiration the way the older woman dressed, her deportment and her gracious manners. She was elegance personified, truly a lady. Her voice was the perfect 'cut-glass' Queen's English accent previously heard only at the cinema, or on the radio and which Mary would like to emulate. Finally, she glanced at Miss Harrington's shoes and wondered about her injury and about the night in the theatre when she and Miranda had escaped with their lives. What a brave and dignified woman, who had gone through so much, experienced tragedy at the Great War, and now was devoting her career to the Civil Service. She seemed so lonely and Mary would have liked to talk to her, but she could not discuss the confidences passed on by Miranda.

As Mary admired and emulated Frances Harrington so did Rita admire and follow Mary. The upheaval of the war had influenced and changed both of their lives as it had so many others. Where would their fate take them next, and ultimately? And where would it take Rita?

CHAPTER 10

A studio flat

In mid-town Colwyn Bay.2009

Liam stumbled out of bed and swore as he crashed into a melange of assorted mismatched mugs, plates and glasses and the remains of a takeaway curry left lying on the bedroom floor on his way to the bathroom. He lunged for the light switch, but realised that the electricity had run out and they needed to go and get credit on the card. He winced with the pain from a headache and sucked in air through his teeth, groaning. He regretted the hangover, caused by the drinking an excess of snakebite the previous night, and now the smell of curry in the fetid air was aggravating it. He and Kayleigh had cashed her giro and gone on a binge before remembering to put credit on the electricity card. He hadn't remembered leaving their tray there on the floor but hey, it could have been there for several days and may remain there. It was hard to see what was what when there was limited electric light and they kept forgetting to get the credit before they ran out of funds, there were so many other priorities.

Kayleigh wasn't keen on housekeeping and why should *he* bother? This wasn't *his* flat. He had met her in the pub a few days ago. They had both been on their own and she invited him home for coffee which seemed like a good idea at the time when seen through an alcoholic haze at the 'Mason's Arms'. They fell into bed that night and the sex may have been good; frenetic, wild, but neither of them had actually remembered very much about it. After the replay the following morning she took a good look at him and decided she liked him rather a lot and invited him to stay here with her. She admitted that there was another man, the owner of all the large leather jackets, and other male clothing around, he who had the tenancy of this flat. While he was incarcerated he would not be able to disturb them at this stage, which was lucky for Liam, who actually had nowhere else to go, except the hostel he had stayed at as a transitory measure, and although he didn't particularly like Kayleigh he drifted into this temporary relationship. He wondered how long he would be able to remain here since this flat was leased to Kayleigh's boyfriend presently doing time at Her Majesty's pleasure, and she was actually just a sub-tenant. The giro should have gone to pay the rent but Kayleigh decided that they should have a night out, forget their troubles and live for the present. She found it difficult to plan ahead, always living for the moment.

The crash had woken her and she moaned. Her head ached badly. *'Babe, where you goin?'* she whined to him as he left the room.

He turned and saw her looking up at him over her chubby shoulder, her tousled bleached blonde hair unkempt and her square face covered with the remains of the previous day's make up. Her dark eyes were bloodshot and smeared with mascara. Tattoos covered her lower back and shoulder blades, with interlacing designs and butterflies. Kayleigh was not young, in her thirties now, but on her unhealthy diet had just managed to keep her figure this long. She was not what Liam had envisaged as an ideal partner, but she was here now, available, useful. *'It's ok babe, I'll be back. I'm not going to work or nothing. As if...'* he laughed sarcastically and left the room. She groaned and turned over burying herself in the none too clean sheets, reminded that she herself had to get up sometime and make the effort to get to her part time job.

Liam staggered from the bathroom to the kitchen, opened the fridge door, *'Better get the electric sorted out,'* he thought, or would the iced up freezer be leaking all over the floor? He grabbed a carton of juice and sniffed to see if it was past its use by date before he drank from it in long draughts. There was nothing else in the fridge but a plastic eye mask, a half empty plastic tray of butter and the remains of a sliced loaf in a plastic bag. He shook an aged carton of cereal, yes miraculously there was some left and he would have had some but no, the milk in the warm fridge was off. He poured it down the sink and ditched the milk carton in the bin then snatched a cigarette from a packet on the worktop, struck a match, lit up and inhaled the nicotine deeply, contemplating.

There were grains of rice scattered on the worktop where the curry had been dished up and a trail of yellow stains from the spices. A half-eaten nan bread lingered in its silver foil bag and he threw it in the swing top bin. He wondered what he was doing here, in this flat, in this town, and thought back to those innocent days when he used to come with his grandfather and stay in guesthouses or B & Bs on holidays with the rest of the family. *'Somewhere on a beach in north Wales,'* Liam reminisced that he always expected his superhero character to appear on the sands during his visits. It would take more than a superhero to get him out of this fix. He had come here with just a small holdall on the spur of the moment, out of nostalgia and had not expected to be in this filthy flat with this woman he hardly knew.

After a series of jobs, which had come to nothing, he had

decided to return to the scene of some of his childhood memories and to stay in a hostel temporarily. He had had a happy childhood. He had been well brought up and he and his sisters had been given everything they needed, and more besides, perhaps too much. The girls were settled and successful. He had had plenty of encouragement and he felt he couldn't now return to his family feeling such a failure. How had he gone so wrong? All the work he had found recently was washing up in a café, but since he had not turned up on time, and once did not go in at all he had been 'let go'. Although he certainly hadn't enjoyed the job that day he had gone to the pub to console himself, drown his sorrow, and bumped into Kayleigh there. If he could use this address and stay a bit longer then he could sign on here, but when would Kayleigh's other half be out, and what would he say if he found him here? Local rumour maintained that he was a violent man, doing time for GBH.

Kayleigh always seemed to get money from somewhere, it was a mystery to him. Her part time job seemed to bring in some, but she never did actually tell him where she worked. She said she sold double-glazing, but she seemed to keep odd hours for the appointments and he had his suspicions. Oh well it wasn't his concern, she wasn't the type of girl he wanted to be with for too long and when he thought of the sort of girl who would be his ideal? Well, why would that type bother with him? But how useful could Kayleigh be in getting him on his feet? She had encouraged him to ask his family for money, but to no avail so far, no, that was not the answer, he didn't want to be found just yet. He had to think of a plan. There were one or two mates around who he had contact with. He knew they were into petty crime, but he didn't care. They were selling drugs on the street and Kayleigh had got him involved in participating. Of course he didn't take much persuasion; he was weak and wanted an easy ride. Once he started to crave more he may have to do a bit of shoplifting to fund his habit. Cocaine was expensive, all the drugs were, especially when you had nothing.

He heard the water running in the bathroom from a noisy cistern needing attention. The mouldy smell and damp emphasized that fact. Minutes later Kayleigh appeared on the threshold and stumbled in to the small kitchen wearing oversized huge fluffy lilac slippers and an old towelling robe of thin worn cotton, with faded cartoon characters of cute little wide eyed animals. The childlike attire belied the worldliness etched on to her face, her tangled peroxide blonde hair was piled up on top of her head now scrunched into a plastic clip, it gave her a couple of inches more height. She was in search of an aspirin and a coffee, and more urgently a fag.

'Oh babe, there's no milk!' she wailed, swinging open the fridge door.' can you go down the road for some, you know I 'ate it... I 'ate black coffee,' she growled in her Mancunian accent.

Liam nodded and obliged, it was the least he could do, after all she was giving him a roof over his head, although it was not hers to give. 'Ere luv.'

She produced a large shabby purse from the kitchen drawer, it was filled with loyalty cards, coupons and old receipts, but hardly any money, and she fumbled among her change for some pound coins. Having gathered enough she thrust them into Liam's hand and said, 'Get me some fags luv, and a scratch card, I'm feeling lucky, I'm lucky to find you babe,' trilling in her gravely smoker's drawl. She sidled up to him, patted the side of his unshaven face, reaching up to kiss him.

He was tall, six foot two and towered over her, and he shrank from her touch. Liam was not in the mood for canoodling. No. He wasn't really keen on Kayleigh, but her company was marginally better than being on his own.

He stepped into his tracksuit bottoms and grabbed a grey hooded sweater from the back of a chair and dragged it over his head, ran his fingers through his longish coppery hair and searched for his trainers under the bed. He didn't mind going, he could do with some air to alleviate his hangover. Yes, fresh sea air was on the doorstep waiting for him. He picked up her keys and called out, *'I'll be right back,'* and slammed the inner door of the apartment on his way through the communal entrance.

Kayleigh shuddered as the leaded glass in the door rattled as it slammed; she swore it would come out one day. She shrugged and tried to put the kettle on, desperate for a coffee, she swung open the fridge door. There was nothing else to drink in the house. Her last ciggy was hanging from her lower lip, and she screwed up the corners of her eyes to avoid the smoke, and then turned to go back into the bedroom.

She looked into the mirror and realised she didn't look her best after the heavy night before, but then she hadn't ever really been a looker, she knew the truth of it, but had got by on her wits, she *had to* because the small vestiges of youthful beauty she had ever had were fading fast. She flopped back down on to the bed. Liam was a real find, she thought, he was from the Wirral, posher than her usual consorts, she would think his family had a bob or two, and although he had no 'career' he had potential and was well bred, unlike Gary. She had to make some decisions before Gary returned from prison.

Liam soon returned from the convenience store with the milk, cigarettes and a couple of scratch cards. 'Match three to win' top prize £100,000. That would be nice and he started to fantasize about what he would do with it. Perhaps he would smarten himself up and return to his family, say he'd had a good job. But he had never met anyone who had won so held out little hope. What they had really bought was a licence to dream because if you had no card or lottery ticket then you couldn't play that escapist game.

CHAPTER 11

With a little help from her friend

Liverpool revisited

Margarita, with a little help from Faye, stepped off the first class carriage on the train coming in to Lime Street and immediately the old memories of her youth came flooding back to her. She had impulsively followed through with her idea to revisit her roots while escaping the hottest time of year in Spain. As a gradual re-introduction to the area she had sat and enjoyed hearing the accents of the people on the train and had surreptitiously and curiously listened in on their conversations, and when she tentatively stepped onto the platform into Lime Street station she recalled the day she had left with her brothers as evacuees destined for Colwyn Bay.

Faye had made reservations for the hotel she had always been booked in to, where else would be fitting in Liverpool? She couldn't imagine, but then she was very out of touch. She was wearing a lightweight tailored suit of soft beige material, comfortable for travelling, with one of her Italian silk scarves at the throat. She and Faye seemed to stand out in the crowd as 'well to do'. She would have preferred to 'blend in' but years of her affluent lifestyle had had the effect that dressing well was effortless now. Faye dealt with the porters, and the Louis Vuitton luggage, monitoring it and pointing it out to the waiting helpers, and then offered her arm for Margarita to lean on; she was stiff from sitting so long on the journey from London where they had stayed overnight in an hotel on Park Lane. They had had business to attend to there after they had flown into Heathrow from Alicante.

Margarita turned to Faye and said, *'Oh dear, I couldn't have managed any of this without you, I had forgotten how tiring the travelling can be, and at my age.'*

Faye was a middle aged widow, efficient, kindly, a real diamond, and well suited as a ladies travelling companion. Since her mother had died the previous year, she had met up with Margarita in Spain and they seemed to gel. She had previous experience of being a PA before she had left her work to care for her mother. Her son was at university so had left home, Faye was doing some kind of historical research herself and was always chatting to Margarita about the war years.

The current arrangement suited both of them down to the ground. Margarita looked on her as something between a surrogate daughter and a sister, and regretted not having had any children, but in those days her career had always come first.

'Oh we'll be fine,' said Faye, *'just as soon as we get ourselves settled into the hotel Rita, don't worry. It's tiring for anyone, so don't you worry about it, you are really great for your age, I do hope I can be half as good as you when I am nearly eighty.'*

They got into a taxi, which soon drew up outside the Hotel. From the brief glimpse of the city Margarita craved another tour by car to visit all the sights; the Liver Building, St George's Hall, to cross the Mersey by ferry. Arriving at this destination, this hotel brought back so many memories for Margarita, of all the dinners, dances and functions she had attended in past decades. Faye had pressing family business of her own to attend to in Liverpool, so after installing themselves in their rooms

Margarita had welcomed the chance for a short nap before going down to the dining room for dinner. Faye had tried to book Margarita a suite, but had to make do with a 'premiere' room, which was huge with high Victorian ceiling and moulded cornices, the view from the window looked down over the city. Chandeliers were hung with crystals and long sheer elegant voile curtains draped the windows. The furniture was large and mahogany. It was still rather grand, as she had always remembered it.

She was enjoying this sortie into her memories, drifting into sweet dreams. She awoke suddenly, wondering for a minute where on earth she was. Then remembered, Faye was busy this evening, it had been agreed that Margarita would dine alone. She arose from the bed and took a shower in the marble en suite bathroom. Then comfortably wrapped in an extremely fluffy towelling robe embroidered with a golden hotel crest, Margarita turned to see which outfit Faye had laid out for her. She really was an excellent travelling companion, everything was to hand and Margarita couldn't have made a better choice herself.

She donned the hyacinth blue two-piece 'costume' as she used to call a ladies suit, with a silk blouse, which was the epitome of low-key elegance, flattering, understated luxury but comfortable, so therefore highly suitable. Then sitting down at the large dressing table she sprayed on some scent with essences of roses and lilies, the most expensive French perfume which had always been her favourite. Taking up the silver backed hairbrush she smoothed back her hair. It had lost the copper-red tones of her youth, but was now pure white, with springy silky waves, and had benefitted from an expert expensive cut. She considered her skin, not bad for her age, she had looked after it, not sat out in the sun too much, having been born a redhead, and didn't feel inclined to resort to a face lift or even botox, it made her shudder. A little subtle eye shadow applied, then the coral pink lipstick she loved.

She hummed to herself strains of the song, that one about the elderly lady who keeps her make up in a jar by the door, and Rita also wondered for whose benefit it was and decided it was for her own. She then produced a silk travelling jewellery pouch from the dressing table drawer and added her double row of graduated pearls with sapphire and diamond jewelled clasp to her ensemble. She noticed a pair of green earrings, and wondered why she had packed them, since she had no outfit of that colour to compliment them. She decided she would give them to Faye. She then clipped on pearl earrings, and of course slipped on her magnificent diamond engagement ring.

Peering into the mirror she hardly recognised herself. Where was the young unsophisticated girl who had been born here in this city years ago and lived with her brothers in the house further down the river, nearer the docks where her father had worked before the war? Where was the popular singer of world renown? Well there was an advantage to this, if she didn't recognise herself then neither would anyone else. She travelled incognito whether she liked it or not. Her days of being mobbed by fans were over now. Those receptionists, just out of school, hadn't known her by her married name when she and Faye had booked in, and anyway they were much too young. But their parents or maybe the grandparents would have known who she was.

She took up her silver grey cashmere pashmina and her pearl grey patent designer handbag and slipped on her expensive, shiny low-heeled shoes. She was ready. She wandered down to the elevator, descended to the lobby and dropped off her key into reception.

It was very quiet at the desk, there was just one receptionist on duty, a pretty girl smartly turned out, immaculately groomed with peachy skin and large dark eyes, she couldn't have been more than twenty.

Margarita smiled sweetly at the girl behind the desk, but again she was unrecognised, just another elderly guest, of whom there were many.

The girl hung up the key, paused momentarily, and noted the number of the room, and the huge diamonds flashing on this guest's finger. *'Good evening Madame Van Royen,'* said the receptionist, *'How can I help you this evening?'*

'I'd like a paper sent to the room in the morning with breakfast, please.'

'Yes of course Madame Van Royen, which one would you like?'

There was a pause while Margarita thought about it.

'The Times? The Telegraph?'

'Oh the Independent... and the Liverpool Post please,' said Margarita, thinking she might make some mischief, by regressing into her former scouse accent while chatting to the girl, who was rather taken aback.

'Yes Madame Van Royen,' the girl looked mystified, then boldly said, *'Oh, you are not Belgian are you?'*

'No dear, I was born near here, in Bootle, my name was Gerard then. I married a Belgian, Van Royen is my married name but I am a widow now.'

'Oh ,Miss Gerard,' said the girl, *'Are you **the** Margarita Gerard, the singer?'*

'Yes dear, I am. I am surprised you have heard of me at your age.'

The girl looked flushed, *'Well my gran has a lot of your CDs and tapes, you have always been one of her favourites, I am so pleased to meet you,'* she gushed. *'Do you think... I mean, would you mind giving me an autograph for my gran?'*

Margarita was secretly delighted to be recognised and

replied, '*Of course I don't mind dear, here, pass me that page and I'll write her a message, what is her name?*'

'*Her name is Elsie, oh she will be thrilled when I tell her I have met you, oh thank you so much*'.

'*Not at all dear, it's my pleasure,*' and Margarita wrote, 'To Elsie with best regards, Margarita Gerard.' She was pleased with herself, she had not been recognised or asked to give an autograph for many a year.

'*And I will make sure the morning papers get to you Miss Gerard, I mean, Madame Van Royen,*' called the receptionist after her as she walked towards the dining room smiling to herself.

In the dining room there were few diners, but it was fairly early, and it was midweek. Perhaps the atmosphere would become more convivial a bit later. After all she had left her quiet home in Spain to see a bit of life, have some company.

She made her way to the table, one of the best, sat down and ordered a cocktail. '*I'll have a Margarita please,*' she asked the good-looking young waiter. One drink wouldn't hurt, she wasn't on any medication, and it felt like a treat.

He came quickly with a tray with a tiny silver flask and a glass with salt crystals glittering like diamonds round the rim. He shook the flask, removed the lid and served the cocktail with a flourish. '*A margarita for Margarita,*' said the handsome young Eastern European.

As he had anticipated, she was not offended, since he had been chatting to the receptionist and had sounded out what sort of guest she would be. She realised, news travels fast on the grapevine and 'below stairs', but was happy and contented to be recognised. She had come 'home'.

Looking down the menu she came to a decision. '*I will have the fois gras to start please, followed by Dover sole, and a selection of vegetables please.*'

'Yes Madame, is that the sole Veronique? Very good, Madame,' and he swept out with a bow.

Margarita enjoyed her meal but then what could she do? She found herself at rather a loose end and lonely once the initial novelty of being back in Liverpool and the experience of being recognised had worn off. She retired to one of the lounges and sat in a large overstuffed brocade easy chair. Popular *musak* played. Orchestral versions of nostalgic Beatle music made her smile... because she too was getting back to the place where she once belonged, she was coming 'home'. A few guests milled around, many were on their way out for the evening.

The waiter brought her coffee and she signed the bill, adding a good tip to the tray then looked deep into her patent handbag for her address book. Who could she visit? She would make some calls when she returned to the room. Faye would not be back for hours, she had private business to attend to, she was visiting family and heaven knows she deserved the time off, she was invaluable in her assistance, indispensable in fact. Perhaps Rita should call her brother and his family. But would they be pleased to hear from her? They were in nearby Hoylake, and she really should let them know she was around. This was all part of her plan for this visit.

Impetuously she picked up her mobile and consulting her address book, dialled the number. But strangely, before finishing she had cold feet and abandoned the call. Returning to her address book she leafed through it intending to return to her brother's number later, in the privacy of her room, after all it was not very private where she sat in the hotel lobby, or was she just procrastinating? Leafing back through the pages of her book she saw there was the number for Hetty, an old stage school friend, yes, she would ring her as soon as she returned to the room. They could have a wonderful gossip about old times, perhaps meet up tomorrow, she had missed Hetty Barnstaple, and she had not heard from her lately.

'*Mrs Barnstaple has gone into a nursing home,*' said the voice at the end of the 'phone, which was Hetty's daughter-in-law. '*She is not at all well, she is due to have an operation tomorrow, and will not be up to receiving visitors for at least a week.*'

Things had changed. There were not many of her friends left. '*Oh I am so sorry to hear that, I didn't realise... and tell her Margarita called and please give her my love. And please, what is the address, I will have some flowers sent to her, and yes, please do give her my love and tell her I hope to see her on my next visit.*'

Margarita dearly hoped she would see Hetty again soon. She noted down the address, promising herself that she would ask Faye to get the flowers sent first thing tomorrow. Then she tried another friend, Shirley, and there was no answer. '*I really should have planned ahead to let people know I was coming,*' thought Margarita, cross with herself at being so remiss. After all it was the height of the summer now, people could be on holiday, but the trip had been arranged spontaneously.

She looked again in the address book and sadly there were one or two people whose names were crossed off, as deceased. That made her even more determined to 'make hay while the sun shone'. Then there were also people like herself who had moved abroad, some for tax reasons, or to enjoy a better climate.

Suddenly, Margarita had a brainwave. Just like Scarlett O'Hara deciding to go home to Tara in *Gone with the Wind*. She would go to Colwyn Bay, how different would that be? How much could it have possibly changed? She hadn't been there for years, that would be a real treat, even if they were to go just for a day's drive out, and she was sure that Faye would enjoy that too. She knew that Faye had an Aunt, a mother-in- law and several other people there who she had been meaning to visit for some time. They often talked of them and agreed that procrastination had been very much the thief of time.

Faye would be delighted with this plan; she knew it, because Faye had been brought up in Colwyn Bay. Their discovery that they had memories of the town in common, and their early conversations about it had created a bond and forged their friendship. They would arrange to hire a car and a driver, she didn't relish getting back on the train and she would need a car to drive around her old haunts. They knew it would not be the way they remembered it but nothing prepared them for the extent to which it had changed. But before that she really *must* call her brother. Returning to her room again she dialled the number and hung on while it connected. It rang out signifying that there was no one at home. A disappointment. However, she had made an attempt, the first step towards reconciliation.

As the years passed, Alex had gone away to Liverpool University. Faye had missed her son, the little boy with rosy cheeks and big blue eyes, who had stood on a kitchen chair to make fairy cakes from his grandmother's and Nainie's recipes. He had turned into a 6ft 2 man with longish hair and a beard, who played loud music, and d-jayed at clubs. She used to say to him as he was growing up. '*Where is that little boy now, is he inside you?*' And she knew he was.

But time had marched on and she knew she had to make changes now. She wouldn't have been able to tie her son to her apron strings even if she had wanted to, but it was nice to visit him at his flat just for one evening, and he had cooked her a meal of lasagne and home baked bread. Faye's husband had died in the '90s, when their son was still very young, and she had supported him through cancer for two years. She had afterwards taken a degree in history to give her an interest, an outlet. It was something she had always wanted to do. When she had gained her degree and Alex had grown up and gone to university she had moved to Spain and rented a villa there, enjoying the sun and carefree time, yet it was an empty and unfulfilling life. She mixed with the expatriate community, playing bridge and attending parties and social events. That was where she and Margarita had first met and they hit it off straight away since they had their roots in common. Both had relocated abroad as widows. Both had been delighted to be able to reminisce about their old town. They would commiserate in its dilapidated state. Faye could see that Margarita, although still sprightly in her 70s needed help and when she had confided in Faye that she was about to advertise, for a personal assistant, companion and carer then Faye asked if she might apply.

'*Oh my dear,*' said Rita, '*I wouldn't have dared to hope that you would consider it. There is nothing I would like more than to see you more often, but we will make a business of it. I know you have a life of your own as well, and I can do a lot for myself still. It's just these damn computers. I struggle to get to grips with answering my correspondence. I still get fan mail you know.*'

They came to an arrangement that suited both. Rita had no children. Faye knew she had relatives in the Wirral but did not want to ask about the row that had estranged them. Rita would tell her if she wanted to, when she was ready. Faye had no parents. She had few relatives left in North Wales, but she liked to keep in touch with those that were left, and of course her in-laws.

It had been Faye's mother in law who had first told her about the wartime years in Colwyn Bay, and about past decades, while chatting over the baking on the kitchen table. The unique contribution of the town had always fascinated Faye, and she wanted to research this further. Why hadn't anyone else told her? She had grown up in the town for goodness sake. Her parents were not there during the war however and hadn't settled there until 1948, but her godparents were, and her parents' friends. It had not been mentioned in school either during the '60s. Still, she had heard that even Churchill was rarely mentioned in schools nowadays. But there were so many people still alive who could tell their stories. History was taken to a different level these days and the stories of the ordinary people were much more valued as a source than they had previously been.

She had discussed her interest with Rita, who was of course an evacuee during wartime. Rita had told her that her life had been dramatically shaped by her move out of the Liverpool poverty, her career had taken off from her dancing tuition and singing in local concerts. She had even met her husband there. He was a little older of course, but they had met up while she was performing in Belgium years later. Their background, the place they had spent their formative years together had provided a great bond, although they had not been friendly or even spoken in those days – just acquaintances. But Rita had told her of how the young Van Royen, a friend of the factory owner's son had stood at the back of the hall in the Castle Hotel watching Rita perform. He was a teenager then, and friendly with a number of girls his own age, but had never forgotten the impact her performance had had on the assembled gathering. In the late forties he had returned after the war to Belgium where he continued to work in the diamond industry and had gone on to great things. After they were married he used to tease her that diamond merchants were *a girl's best friend*. During their courtship he had given her diamonds almost as big as those lavished on Elizabeth Taylor by Richard Burton. He knew how she felt about him. She had ignored the attentions of famous stars of the day for him.

From the cosy chats with Rita and the other expatriates Faye had realised she had a special interest in recording the oral histories of her friends, the older generation, and felt passionate that such information should not be lost. Rita relayed what old Norah had told her and empathised with Faye's enthusiasm for the preservation of memories.

Faye wanted to visit her elderly aunt who had been employed at the diamond factory and also with the Ministry of Food in wartime and had forgotten to mention it. She had thought no one would be interested. Rita had expressed an interest in revisiting Colwyn Bay. What a wonderful opportunity for them to go together. Faye was apprehensive about what Rita would think of the town, how it had changed, how disappointed she would be, but Rita was adamant and they could travel together. Rita had no ties there these days, and few contacts – or so she thought.

CHAPTER 12

'Resurgam' (I will rise again)

'The Castle Hotel revisited'

L iam sat at the window smoking. Rain ran down the pane relentlessly confining him to the small shabby flat. For entertainment Liam's options were financially challenged. He just wanted the simple pleasure of going for a walk, to stroll around on memory lane and to reminisce about his holidays in the eighties, to revisit in his mind all that had happened in his family and try to make sense of it.

§His Grandad used to say that he always got his best ideas when he was out walking. Liam had seen enough so far since returning to the town to know that he was due to suffer some disappointment. Casting his mind back to better days the realisation dawned on him that often it was better to travel only in one's mind, clinging on to the good aspects, glamourizing, forgetting conveniently what was not so good about a place in which he had stored up and harboured memories like treasure. He thought of his young nephew and speculated how the children of today's generation would look back, and concluded that it would probably be the same for them, they wouldn't know the difference. They never even had the chance to see the dinosaurs in the park.

In the 1980s Liam treasured an image of a laughing toddler

grasped in his Grandad's arms, and had revelled in the huge growling dinosaur replicas at Eirias Park. Liam's view was that this town just wasn't what it had been in his childhood, in the span of his short life, twenty five years it had deteriorated, everyone said so, but it was a trend all over the country. It seemed from what he had read in the papers that other towns had been 'regenerated'; and it was now the turn of this town to be 'spruced up' enough to attract some visitors, some income or just to be improved for the local population. He wasn't quite ready to get involved in the many projects suggested, needing to focus on his own predicament first in his hierarchy of needs. He was obsessed by finding the 'Castle Hotel', a Victorian building of quarry stone, which he remembered being near the sea, he hoped I had not been demolished like so many others. The rain had subsided and he was ready for his walk.

Kayleigh had wanted to come with him, and there she was in her unsuitable heels and short skirt, hot to trot around after him She had fallen more than a little in love with him she had to admit, and was no longer intent on just using him. He could see this and did nothing to reciprocate in their relationship. If she would just stand back, be a little more unavailable he may have been remotely interested. Not only did she did fancy a future with him, but her feelings had spiralled beyond her control and her usual scheming plans. In reality the time for Gary, her former lover, and tenant of the flat, to come out of jail was drawing dangerously near and she would then have to come to a decision, so for now she would have to go along with this funny idea of Liam's, looking at an old derelict hotel. She did not relate to Liam's feelings about seeking out the past, not that he had confided much in her. There was no room in her life for the luxury of sentimentality; she focussed on her daily needs, and in her order of such her priority was for the basics in life. She knew that 'The Castle' has been closed down and boarded up; she had read about it in the local paper while she sat waiting for her takeaway curry. The hotel had gone bust due to lack of business a few years ago, it had not attracted any tourists for whatever reasons, so it had been empty for some time. She had never been inside there while it was open for functions; it wouldn't have been her cup of tea. It seemed to her that this had been a venue for the elderly, for the *University of the Third Age*, or for the Women's social clubs to meet or even for holding funeral receptions. None of these events would have interested her even if she had been invited.

Kayleigh scuttled alongside with her short skirt and odd gait, trying to keep up, clicking in her kitten heels next to Liam striding out athletically in his trainers. She tried to strike up a conversation with him. '*So ... who came here then in those days?*' she asked.

He answered tersely, '*My Grandad, parents and sisters.*' Liam was not particularly keen to disclose much about his family to her.

'Well *why do you want to go there now, babe?*'

Liam ignored her, she wouldn't understand. They approached the entrance with iron gates set back a bit from the road. High wooden panels enclosed the plot, some of which had become unsecured, foliage spilled over and through the gaps promising a haven for wildlife beyond. The gardens had had time to 'mature' and had become very overgrown with a quantity valerian is two shades of deep red and pink, and a myriad of butterflies were encircling the purple buddleia, thriving among the oaks and overgrown conifers. Droplets of water sparkled on the large leaves and rolled off splashing down as Liam shook the fences.

A large sign proclaimed, '*By order, keep out, danger demolition site'* both in English and in Welsh. Liam had a quick look around him then recklessly ignored this and bent back a panel to slip inside and strode ahead with determination, pushing the weeds aside. He had no fear for his or Kayleigh's safety, and little conscience to tell him that he really shouldn't be doing this, it was trespassing.

A creature scuttled away in the wet undergrowth, he suspected it was a rat so he didn't say anything to Kayleigh believing she would have had hysterics. What did she want to come for anyway? They were *his* memories, and she wasn't a part of this, he really didn't want to share them with her. She had followed him and they found their way, dodging and diving among the tall, out of control shrubs around the back to the kitchen entrance until they came to a boarded up door hanging off its hinges, some vandals had been here before them making it easier for them to gain access.

'*Babe, let's not go in, it might be dangerous, and it will be dirty,*' whined Kayleigh.

'*Why didn't she shut up,*' thought Liam. '*Dirty? What gave her – of all people – the right to be so prissy, she had foregone that particular privilege due to her lack of housekeeping skills, and low standards of hygiene?*' It would be him who would get the job of going to the launderette with their dirty clothes, while she was on one of her so called 'appointments' for selling double glazing. He was determined to go in anyway, he had made up his mind, he was curious and wanted to revive his memories.

The door gave way easily with one push of his shoulder and he found himself in a dark corridor. He got his lighter out of his pocket and when satisfied that he couldn't smell gas at all he lit it. Further evidence that others had been here before them was to be seen here, a candle and tea lights on a windowsill. Great, they still had a little wick left in them. He lit the first candle, it cast a mysterious glow on the scene immediately, it flattered both their appearances, softening their features, and their mood mellowed as he handed the light to Kayleigh, who giggled saying *'I feel like Jane Eyre... oh Mr Rochester!'* He was impressed by her cultural reference; he hadn't thought she had it in her to know of such things. She must have seen it on the telly, he couldn't imagine her reading the Bronte novels.

'Well then, don't bloody well set fire to the place. You do know the ending don't yer?' thinking, well she is a bit mad like Rochester's first wife, Bertha Mason. Then his thoughts turned to the inscription Jane Eyre leaves on her school friend Helen's grave when she places the stone with the word "Resurgam" (I will rise again). He was reminded then of the mosaic of a submarine of that name at the neighbouring Rhyl museum. It had been suggested that it should have been yellow reflecting the links with the area where it was built, not far from Liam's home. That original vessel had been sunk in 1880 off the coast and eventually discovered by a diver.

After successful trials in the East Float at Wallasey, it was planned that Resurgam should make her way under her own power from Birkenhead to Portsmouth for a demonstration to the Royal Navy.

However, during the voyage mechanical problems caused the crew to dock at Rhyl for repairs. Once completed, the crew set sail at night in a high wind, towed by the steam yacht Elphin, which had been bought to act as a tender. The Elphin developed engine problems and the Resurgam's crew transferred to her to assist. Because the entry hatch on could not be fastened from outside, the submarine began to ship water and the tow rope broke under the added weight, sinking in Liverpool Bay off Rhyl on 25 February 1880.

Liam had returned to a place which had meaning for him.

Quickly coming to his senses and the present issues he searched his pocket then assembled some tea lights on an old cracked plate, and lit those for himself to carry. If only he had thought of getting a torch, but they had little money except for essentials like ciggies and alcohol, and other means of getting through life. He was still awaiting his giro since registering at the benefits office using Kayleigh's address. She was unusually quiet now, thank goodness she had shut up. He suspected she was scared, and she hadn't even been aware of the rat.

She followed Liam down the corridor concentrating on keeping her candle safely lit (being terrified of the dark it was essential for her well-being), through to a hallway. The kitchen was off to one side and they went through a sort of scullery, with Belfast sinks. He glanced at them and thought they would be worth something, how could the site managers have missed those? It would be a pity if they were trashed, but a bit heavy to carry away. Anyway they were not his to take, so that was an end to it, he was trying not to be a thief. Then he pushed a door, which swung on rusty hinges giving a creak reminiscent of the sound effects of the 'Bates motel'.

Liam curiously ventured further on, Kayleigh bravely shadowing him, her heels no longer clicking on the damp felt underfoot. She would have been too afraid to turn back on her own now from this other world they had entered. Finally they found themselves in the main hallway, there was some 1970's style red swirly patterned carpet remaining, shabby and ripped and very dirty. They looked up the sweeping staircase and he decided it would be better to investigate the downstairs rooms first. The place smelled damp, water was obviously entering at many points of damage. This building was earmarked for demolition but the developers planning to build the luxury retirement flats on site had gone bust and the project had been put on hold pending legal tangles. It seemed that it had been cleared in a hurry because there was still some furniture remaining. In the lounge the actual bar still stood with the liquor optics in place, sadly for Kayleigh no friendly drop was to be found, but she was becoming more interested when one of her favourite topics, alcohol, was in sight. There were no tables or chairs left, but the window seat was integral, in place, even with cushions on it, although ripped with the stuffing spilling out.

Liam scanned the room remembering past times and he could almost superimpose them on this scene. He visualised days gone by when he was a young boy, back in the late eighties, and allowed in the bar for a bottle of orange juice and a packet of crisps with his grandfather and sisters, because they were residents. He walked through to the empty dining room, and imagined the scene with white starched tablecloths, linen napkins and all of the family sitting up straight in their best clothes and on their best behaviour, their faces shining with happiness, sampling new foods they hadn't tried before, having happy family conversations around the table. Granddad Jim would be telling them about the town in the war years, about when the daughter of the house to which he had been evacuated had taught Rita to dance. Another layer of the past seemed to peel back as Liam imagined his Granddad's childhood here in the town. Jim had brought them to this very hotel and had told them of his own wartime memories. 'The Castle' had been in use by the Ministry in the 1940s. The teenage girl at his evacuee home, through her connections with a dancing school, had brought him and his sister to see a concert staged in the ballroom. Jimmy could imagine it, and now so could Liam although he wasn't born until the 1980s. Mary would be dancing, and Aunt Margarita as a little girl started to join in after having some coaching from the older girl. Granddad Jimmy had related the story of how he had seen her debut performance at a concert in this very hotel during wartime, and they were all so surprised to find out she had a wonderful gift and talent. Margarita used to sing popular songs of the 1940s whenever they visited her when Liam was a boy, recreating an atmosphere for his grandfather Jimmy.

Liam turned on his heel, he had to go and see the ballroom right away, he burst in dramatically through the double doors, it was exactly as he had remembered it, but so much smaller. A new layer of visualisation of Liam's impression of his own childhood days flashed before his eyes. Tricks of the mind overwhelmed him and he was overcome with nostalgia, which he didn't want to share, not with Kayleigh, she wouldn't understand. The music started to echo in his head, what was it his aunt used to sing, he tried to remember... the list ran through his mind. Among others there was the traditional 'Home Sweet Home', almost like a hymn, and then the song his home football team adopted. On these last two poignant memories he started to tremble with emotion. He missed his family so much, he wished there hadn't been that stupid row with Margarita, and they assumed he had been the cause of it. How he wished he hadn't been so rude to them all. How could he ever get back to his former life? He felt he was becoming emotionally unstable and suspected that the use of drugs had exacerbated this. How had it come to this? He wanted life to go back to the way it had been, but he did not want to admit his failure to his family. Was there a way back for him? Would they forgive him for being such a disappointment to them? Did they still love him?

He reached for his phone from the pocket in the leg of his green cargo pants and photographed this scene, although who he would share it with he did not know. In the background Kayleigh had followed him and was now was sitting on an old upholstered chair with the stuffing tumbling out. This must have been deemed too worthless to take from the site when it was cleared, yet escaped the skip. She was rubbing her foot complaining of her blisters, she had walked too far already that day. *'Liam'*, she said looking through a gap she had rubbed in the whitewashed windows. *'There is a woman standing out there by the gap in the fence? She has been staring over here! Do you think she knows we are in here, what shall we do?'*

'Dunno?' he answered, then *'Yes I can see her... with long dark hair?'* Liam wondered if he had gone too far by coming here. He swallowed the lump in his throat and said with fake cheerfulness.

'When she's cleared off we'll go. Let's go and buy a bottle of cider and a scratch card. Before these candles go out, yeah? What d'ye say? And next time maybe we'll try to get into the pier pavilion'.

Kayleigh look horrified at the prospect but knew better than to argue with him, she wouldn't be going there, was he mad? Then he turned and took one more look around the room before the candle flickered and went out, thinking to himself that he *would* return here. Kayleigh, an atavist, was all for his first plan she had had enough of his reminiscing for the day and wanted to get back to her comfort zone.

CHAPTER 13

Winners and losers – and losers

There was more in the paper again this week about the robbery at the petrol station and Liam was reading it over the shoulder of the man in front of him in the queue at the Co-op. He recognised the name of the person who had been arrested for the robbery at knifepoint. He was one of the influx who had been attracted to living in a 'House of Multiple Occupation' on benefit. He was just an acquaintance, but one from the underclass who had supplied drugs to Kayleigh and himself at intervals.

Kayleigh sidled up to Liam in the queue with a large bottle of cider and whispered hoarsely to him to remind him to buy some ciggies and a scratch card. She looked down into the basket and saw he had picked up some soup and beans, eggs too, butter and milk, bread – and even a bottle of bleach and toilet paper. Why didn't she think of it? The old man in front with the newspaper suddenly thought of something he needed and darted to one side to pick it up, hoping to get back into his place in the queue. His memory really was not as reliable as it used to be, and if he hadn't just thought of this item he would have to return again to the shop later. Kayleigh took this opportunity to dart ahead and say, *'Two scratch cards please. Number 7 cards, and twenty Richmond an all.'*

Liam lifted the wire basket up to the counter and paid for

everything in it, in addition to the items Kayleigh had put in it. He had at last received his giro now and had enough left this week to pay for groceries and was happy to pay her share too, as he was dossing in Kayleigh's place. Anyway, she wanted to go for a session at the tanning salon. It was her priority and what Kayleigh wanted she usually got, without a thought for the future. Then they would have virtually no money left for the rest of the week. They would have to think of a way of getting some.

The old man who had forgotten his item turned back and with dismay realised he had lost his place in the queue, sighed in resignation thinking, '*They could have let me back into the queue. They have no respect,*' fuming, and waited for them to pack. He also wanted a scratch card, a little luxury he sometimes allowed himself, and the chance to dream about how he could help his family if he were to win a big prize. He noticed how shabby and unkempt they both were, and he disliked her butterfly tattoos which were visible through the spaghetti straps on her top. '*Disgraceful!*' he thought. He wouldn't like to see his grandchildren in that state. *They* were working, not layabouts like these two who he had recognised from other occasions.

The young couple had taken up their plastic bags and left, Alf had glared at them on his way outside the shop and he scratched his number 7 card immediately, because if he had a small win he could claim it from the shopkeeper straight away without having to make a return trip to the shop. '*Oh ten pounds!*' He was delighted. He thought to himself. '*Those two scallies did me a favour just now. They would have had this card if they had waited their turn. They looked as if they need this more than I do. I wonder if their cards brought them any joy.*'

They looked carefree today, they had had a little money in their pockets to spend, but give them a few days and they would be skint again, it would be a different story. Liam was oblivious of the fact that the old gentleman was annoyed at them taking his place in the queue. He and Kayleigh decided to walk back via the promenade; it was a glorious day, which helped to lift their spirits. They sat on a bench overlooking the pier, drinking fizzy drinks from a couple of cans and smoking. Liam thought about the old hotel they had been to, and had contemplated moving in there, but pragmatically realised there would be no running water or heating. He would consider going there on his own another time when he wanted to get away from Kayleigh's mindless chatter, so he could be alone to indulge his reminiscence and to try to think straight, and plan what his future would be.

Liam tried to talk to her about the old days, because in the absence of his relatives, and without friends in this town, who else could he tell? but he knew she really wasn't interested. He tried asking her some questions about her background, but she didn't even want to talk about that. All she said was that she had been named for some aviator in the district. This sounded odd to him but she didn't have any further explanation why she should be named after Sir George Cayley who had connections to the area of Rhos, and whose family had been landowners in the nineteenth century, but Kayleigh did not claim to have any connection.

The eponymous song which may have given the inspiration for her name was a number two UK hit for a British rock band in 1985. The single was kept from the number one spot by a charity single (which was also his football team song) that summer. He knew this because he was born around that time, and had been told of it. He was 25. But she was too old to be named for it then , she must have been one of the first Kayleighs. He gathered there had been rough times for her, brought up by her grandmother, and she didn't want to drag up the past. They smoked, and since the conversation had dried up he remembered that they should scratch their cards. He offered both of them to her and she hesitated to pick one, then chose the other, then scratched it with a gelled chipped burgundy coloured nail. Kayleigh uttered an expletive in disgust,' what a waste of *a quid! And I've got two symbols for a grand' ere. What about yours Liam?*' She looked over at him. '*Hang on*' said Liam still scratching with a coin. He looked up at her and an expression of shock came over his face.

'*I've won,*' he said flatly, emotionless. How cool was he?

'*Good job I went before that old bloke in the shop, I've seen 'im in there loads of times, he always buys that same sort of scratch cards, number 7,*' Kayleigh said. '*What d'ye get, a tenner? Or is it twenty five?*' Liam started to feel sorry for the man in the queue in the shop.

'*No Kayleigh. I mean I have won five thousand quid!*' He must have been in shock and disbelief because he had no reaction, not like her. He needed time for it to sink in. But he thought, was five thousand quid really going to get him out of mess he was in? Half of it would be hers anyway, as they had a tacit agreement that they would share. She shrieked, and her cries were carried away by the wind and the large waves crashing against the rusty promenade railings. She jumped up and despite her feet hurting in her unsuitable shoes, did a little war dance on the spot, threw her arms around his neck and kissed him. He was still sitting down so this was achievable for her, and unavoidable for him. '*Ahhhhhh, I never thought this would 'appen!*' she presumed he would share it with her.

Unable to defer her gratification she shrieked, '*Let's go an gerrit then.*' He answered her calmly and quite seriously, wisely in the knowledge that this was not in any way an answer to all their problems. '*We can't babe, look on the back here,*' he was scrutinizing the ticket, squinting in the sunlight, struggling to read the small print. *'You must be sixteen, yeah fine... be in possession of the ticket...* he would guard it closely until he had the money in his hand... but, *'You can claim prizes of between £1 to £100 any retailer, but over that up to £50,000 you have to tell the retailer or call up this number on the back. Kayleigh, have you got any credit on your phone?'*

'No babe, we could try a payphone, d'ye know where there is one that's working? They're usually all trashed. I expect the ones in Rhos-on-sea would be working.' She was in a fever to get their money. But how would this really change their lives?

* * *

They both imagined for a few moments. Kayleigh's fantasy was all about clothes shopping, a bit of 'bling' of course, and maybe another tattoo... oh and an 'oliday somewhere 'ot. She could already visualise herself and Liam at Manchester airport in the bar before the flight drinking cocktails. She realised that she had to get a passport first, that would involve a trip to Liverpool. She wondered if Liam would take her to introduce her to his family while they were there. Liam? He was thinking about a new decent outfit, the few clothes he had with him were shabby, and if he looked decent he then would pay the train fare home to the Wirral where, on arrival, he would invent a plausible explanation of where he had been. Of course, some of the money would be Kayleigh's – if she had had the winning card surely she would have shared it with him? Or would she? He looked at her, his eyes narrowing as he tried to guess what was going on in her mind and he could imagine her shallow aspirations. But there was something more urgent she required, and soon! She wanted a fix.

He went back to the issue of claiming the money. He thought it would be possible to get it from the post office. He had a driving licence as ID, but it was a lot of money to keep *'under the mattress'* especially someone else's mattress. He didn't want to put the money into his bank because he was overdrawn. Also, round here if they were seen to have come into money then news would travel, and the rent arrears would swallow up a huge chunk of it. He would have to give this some thought.

Kayleigh had already hatched her own plan. She knew it may be tricky getting the money, and she was not strong on delayed gratification, but she had ways. She could go to a loan shark and borrow on the strength of it. She didn't think for one minute of the punishing repayment. Loan sharks didn't care about the consequences of their clients' actions, they should come with a government health warning stamped on them. But in spite of the fact she knew what could happen she was prepared to go ahead with a loan. Yes, she would do that.

They decided to head back for home, put their food in the fridge first, and then Kayleigh wanted to go through the shopping centre, just 'window shopping babe' and to look in the window of the travel shop on the way. She needed to make a sly visit to a dealer she knew who would advance her some goods on the strength of their windfall. Liam was wary of her. He put the winning card in his nylon wallet and crunched the Velcro firmly shut, with a worried look on his face.

After they had been back to their flat they decided to go separate ways in town, after all she said, they would need to look in different shops. She trusted him to take the ticket with him. Unbeknown to her Liam got the bus to Rhos-on-sea and went straight to the post office there, where they weren't known in the area, then he would put the money in his rucksack, buy her a present, perhaps a set of luxury sheets in the linen shop there, (

she would like satin) then think carefully the best way to handle this. He didn't want to row with her, because she had been putting him up and he genuinely was developing some feelings for her. On the other hand, if they split up through arguing over what they would spend the money on, well... she knew some unsavoury characters, as well as Gary.

He knew he had to get back to her as soon as possible, and hoped she hadn't put the word about too much. He told her to keep schtum. It wasn't a lot of money in the scheme of things, but more than they had ever seen. He would feel unsafe carrying it about.

* * *

Kayleigh looked for Jay, a crony of her partner Gary in one of the insalubrious pubs in the area. She knew where to find him, and she headed there even before being tempted by looking in any of the shops. She wanted to avoid Liam for the moment in case he didn't approve. She reached the pub on the corner and pushed past a group of rough looking smokers who had gathered on the doorstep. Discordant music penetrated the air. Inside Jay was immediately identifiable as he sat on a bar stool, in a vest displaying his ugly tattoos.

A pint of bitter stood on the bar in front of him. He looked pleased to see her as he turned his alcoholic gaze towards her, swaying and trying to focus. *'Kayleigh, me old mate. Where've ya been?* said Jay. *'Yer know I'm always here of a dinner time, yer can always find me ere...'* An expression came over his face as he suddenly had an idea. *'Ave yer cum to tell me Gary is outta the nick?'*

This would not be good news for him, since he had shared Kayleigh's sexual favours with Gary, but Kayleigh had set her sights on Liam now, and she wouldn't be keeping company with

Jay any more, although she hadn't yet decided how she would handle Gary.

'No not yet, said Kayleigh. But it won't be long now... Erm, I was wondering... and looked around conspiratorially... can you get me something?'

'Well Kayleigh, as its you... anything is possible,' he lowered his voice... 'at a price.' The price she had in mind this time did not involve taking off her clothes. 'But Kayles, you DO know that Gary is on the way back from Strangeways don't yer? Yer, 'e left this mornin an ee give me a call not long ago.'

Kayleigh went white despite her fake tan and as soon as she had collected what she came for she fled in a race to get to the flat before Gary.

CHAPTER 14

Return to our Roots, The Journey

A few days later as she breakfasted in her room alone Rita read the *Liverpool Post*. Sadly she noticed another old friend's obituary. So hoping to find more cheerful news she turned to another paper but instead was shocked to read: *'Liverpool has been named England's most deprived area in a government report highlighting the most underprivileged parts of the country.'* The words had jumped out of the page at her. She read on. *'The report, compiled by the Department for Communities and Local Government, ranks all of England's three hundred and fifty four local authorities in terms of deprivation, a measure based on factors that include crime, the availability of education, standard of housing and quality of health, and the income of residents.'*

She found this depressing, and questioned how it could possibly be worse in Liverpool nowadays than it was for *her* there as a child? Or her ancestors, who had come over from Ireland during the potato famine! Then she turned to her hotel brochure to read a contrasting view of the city: *For the most visited attractions, go to the stunning Albert Dock...* Oh yes she knew the Albert Dock, as it had been, but now... curious she read on in another tourism leaflet: *It showcases the best of the city in a 'World Heritage', waterfront setting. Situated in the largest group of Grade I listed buildings in the UK – 1.25 million square feet – and was built to the design of engineer and architect Jesse Hartley. Plans were first* submitted in 1839, approved in 1841 and the Dock was officially opened on 30 July 1846 by Prince Albert. She vaguely remembered the old docks in the nineteen thirties, where her father worked before he was called up in the army.

The Albert Dock houses two hotels as well as many award winning visitor attractions including 'Tate Liverpool', the famous 'Beatles Story', 'Merseyside Maritime museum', 'International Slavery Museum', and right on our doorstep the 60 metre high Echo Wheel located on the Piazza outside the Echo Arena.

Albert Dock was the first enclosed, non-combustible dock warehouse system in the world and the first structure in Britain to be built entirely of cast iron, brick and stone. In 1848 the world's first hydraulic warehouse hoists were installed. The Dock was built to accommodate sailing ships with up to 1,000 tons' cargo capacity but by the turn of the century only seven per cent of ships using the Port were sailing ships. The Dock's days were numbered and it was finally closed in 1972.

It was coming back to her now, her friends had discussed this briefly in letters, albeit only once a year enclosed in Christmas cards. But she had not fully taken it in. Living abroad she had really lost touch with the city of her roots. She continued reading: *The refurbishment of Albert Dock was carried out by the Arrowcroft Group, through its subsidiary, the Albert Dock Co Ltd. Plans were prepared in 1982, work began in 1983 and the first phase was opened in 1984 in time for the arrival of the Tall Ships Race and the International Garden Festival. The official re-opening ceremony was performed by Prince Charles on 24 May 1988. The original building cost was £514,475-8s-1d. The present day insurance valuation of the buildings, however, is in excess of £250 million. http://www.albertdock.com/history/*

How different was her birthplace from the way she remembered it as a child? How much she had missed by being abroad, travelling for much of her life, and now living in Spain, and she wished she had been better informed. She should have asked people to send on newspapers to her. Momentarily she thought perhaps she should have stayed there, or at least visited more often. No, of course, when she originally left she had no choice. She was evacuated, she was only nine years old, it was wartime and what had become of her youngest brother?

Going back to her reading she saw that now that there was the *Fame Academy* – a bursary scheme set up after the first series of an eponymous TV reality show, which generated one million pounds from record sales and phone lines.

She read on: *The bursary aims to develop new musical talent throughout the UK by supplying musical instruments to young people between the ages of 11 and 15 with a passion for music and supporting the musical education of promising students aged between 16 and 30. The first stage of the bursary will fund these two schemes, which will give away more than 150 instrument grants worth up to £1,200 and five education bursaries worth £12,500 per year for the next three years. Paul McCartney said: 'It is a fantastic way to give really talented young musicians throughout the UK the chance to develop their musical skills.'*

'The Fame Academy Bursary has been looking for young people aged from 11 to 30 who are exceptionally talented and passionate about making music. The award could include dance, vocal, performance.'
http://www.bbc.co.uk/pressoffice/pressreleases/stories/2003/10_october/03/academy_mccartney.shtml

She understood better than most what it was to have that burning ambition. She had made it before the Mersey scene. She had recently heard there were thousands of young people now who wanted to gain fame through their singing and performance. Would her philanthropy help this cause? She had to think about her will, since she was estranged from close relatives and those friends she still had were already comfortably off.

From her further breakfast-time reading it seemed there was plenty around this location to entertain her. But it was the height of the season and she would prefer to be at her distance, and wanted something a little quieter. Maybe she would return in the autumn or spring when the children were back at school. She hadn't realised how taxing the trip would be, hadn't visited this city since she was very much younger and didn't want to queue for attractions or coffee shops at her age. As an alternative, what of the North Wales countryside, cool and serene, and nostalgic.

She looked at her wristwatch, platinum with diamonds set all around the face, then covered it again with the sleeve of her cardigan. She was ready for an early start. Although she was twenty years older than Faye she was always ready first. It was time Faye came to her room now. The car was booked to take them wherever they wanted to go. She sighed with relief as Faye vivaciously and cheerily entered the room, with her hair damp. *'Good Morning Rita. I have been for an early morning swim in the hotel pool.'*

Phil turned up exactly on time in his sleek grey Mercedes, although it was not a new one. This car was not too *high profile*. Rita was beyond impressing, she had had more than her share of that in her days of stardom. Now she just wanted a comfortable ride and not to be noticed and pursued, not that she was expecting that to happen. She had surfeited on adoration. Faye and Rita waited to be notified by reception that the car had arrived and together they stepped out of the lobby.

'Good morning ladies,' breezed Phil. He was a very dapper man, a retired policeman, now working for the taxi company. He looked at Rita, puzzled, as if he knew her from somewhere, but couldn't place where. In his early sixties his memory was not as

good as it had been. It would come back to him; he made a mental note to do more Sudoku to exercise his brain. He then gallantly ushered them to the kerbside and opened the passengers' doors at the back, first seeing Rita in then glancing admiringly at Faye as she elegantly swept her slim legs into the car before he closed the door on her side.

They exchanged pleasantries, decided on the exact destination, when this was done, a brief chat settled the ladies into reveries of their own, glancing at their magazines, and the tourist brochures they had picked up at the reception. Phil kept looking at them in his mirror still intrigued, and trying to remember who the older lady was. Every mile travelled brought back memories for Rita, from her evacuee days up until the visits with her brother's family. Faye had been there more recently, but it was no less nostalgic for her. They had both spent their formative years in North Wales in whose hillsides where they could always count on a warm welcome.

There was a copy of the *North Wales Weekly News* left on the seat, which they noticed as they had stepped in, it had been left there thoughtfully by Phil and they read it avidly seeking out connections. He had been told they wanted to go to Colwyn Bay and he wondered why they would want to. It had seen better days, with the pier derelict and re-paving of the main streets in progress at the height of the season. '*These ladies must have relatives there,*' he thought to himself. '*That must be it*'. No, not relatives but a relationship with the town, and memories.

Meanwhile both Rita and Faye were very keen to look through this paper and Rita resolved to arrange to get this sent to her after she returned home so that she could keep in touch with what was going on in the area. Faye thought she would look it up more often on the website, but it wasn't quite the same as having it in your hands.

The newspaper and the journey brought up memories for both of them. Rita thought of the neighbour she used to visit next door to the Jones' family when she was a child during the war. Norah was an old lady then and must have been born in the 1860s, thought Rita, reckoning it up, as she remembered all the stories she had heard from the interesting old lady. *'More people should tell **real** stories to children,'* she thought to herself, *'otherwise how would these tales survive? And probably they would be more beneficial to them too as an influence.'*

Of course the children would have to have an interest, and to listen properly and remember them. Rita had not brought up any children herself and did not realise how capricious they could sometimes be, although her brother's grandchildren had always listened attentively and politely to her tales. She knew little about her own family history, just that there was an Irish background.

Her own Great Grandparents had in fact come over during the potato famine, as had so many others finding refuge in droves and populating Liverpool. Norah's family as she remembered it had always lived in Colwyn Bay, and Norah had watched the progress as much of it had been built, since most of the houses in Britain had been built between the wars. She had had a wealth of information, and wouldn't Faye have loved to hear it all. Now if only Rita could remember more!'

'This is why I should have written more down' she thought crossly to herself. Some of this information could be researched in books. She had remembered being told that the Romans had occupied and travelled through North Wales, with Sempronius marching with his legions towards Anglesey. Yes they had had a great presence there, evident by the many items which had been found locally as proof. There had been coins and even an amphora, which had lain unrecognised in someone's garden

before being recognised and transferred to the library showcase. The most vivid tales which she could remember and which stood out dramatically in her memory were of the about the Prince, Madoc, who had sailed in 1170 to discover America three hundred years before Columbus. Madoc, one of the nineteen children of King Owain Gwynedd had set out on the Gwennan Gorn from a harbour in Rhos on sea and landed in Alabama, it was said there had been proof. Then there were stories about the castle on the hill, Llys Euryn, and a site which was believed to be home to the ancestors of Henry the Eighth. The school for young black students was not well known, they had been brought over from the Congo in the C19th, by a missionary? Those poor Africans were to learn skills which they could teach when they returned home, but sadly they died of influenza in the harsh climate which they had never known before.

The Mercedes was getting near to Penmaenhead now. Faye had asked the driver, with Rita's agreement, to come off the A55 at Abergele, as she had wanted to go on a particular route. She was reading from a brochure. *In 1399 King Richard II of England was ambushed by Henry Bolingbrook's men at Penmaenhead.*

She turned to Rita, '*Did you know that?*'

Rita shook her head, and asked, '*Why was he here?*'

Faye answered, '*Returning from Ireland,*' then continued, '*Richard was deposed and after incarceration in Pontefract Castle and died in mysterious circumstances. The traitor Bolingbrook became King Henry IV of England.*' The act of treachery on Penmaenhead was to encourage Owain Glyndwr's rebellion that spread throughout Wales and the border lands causing turmoil for the next decade and more, and led ultimately to the Wars of the Roses.

But as fascinating as they were, the legendary events of past centuries were not why Faye wanted to stop. They pulled up near to a new housing development, still in progress. *'There used to be a hotel here'*, said Faye. *'It was called 'Seventy Degrees'. All the angles of the building were at seventy degrees, even the carpets were cut at that angle. Most unusual! I'll tell you something hilarious, a lady who didn't understand the degree sign circle used to call it seventy percent! – or was that because of the prices they charged?'*

Rita and Phil chuckled at this. *'If it had been left standing it would have been a curiosity, representing the architecture of the 1970s. The best thing about it was the view. People loved going there for that.'* There was indeed a fabulous view from this spot. This was something children arriving on their holidays, or anyone returning home to the Bay, seeing this approach they would never forget. Faye remembered to herself that her family used to sing a particular song when they reached this point of the journey in their old Jowett car in the 1950s. It had been an old favourite of her parents. But her younger brother used to call it *'Now is the wawr'*instead of *'hour'*. the little boy not knowing that *wawr* was the welsh word for *dawn*.

'I remember that one,' said Rita, *'It became a hit in about 1948, sung by Frank Sinatra and Bing Crosby but I think it was Gracie fields who sang it before they did. The melody was a Swiss Cradle song, with Maori words added. Gracie's driver taught it to her on a tour of New Zealand in 1945, so it is quite appropriate that your family always sang it in the car.'*

Phil, listening in to their conversation, suddenly remembered why Rita was familiar to him, she had been a favourite singer of his own parents back in the 50s when he was a child.

Faye stared at her, stunned. *'Goodness me Rita, you are a mine of information where songs and music are concerned.'* Then began to tell Rita and Phil something else interesting about the view they had just seen on the approach to the town.

But Rita had stopped listening, she was thinking of her travels to New Zealand, and in particular to Australia, years ago. She had heard of Cosmic Ordering, and thought there was a Maori connection to it. She silently wished hard, putting in her order with the Cosmos. She felt apprehensive about going to Colwyn Bay, and the memories it would bring up. Faye mentioning her own young brother caused memories of Rita's brothers to surface from the past and she found it hard to deal with them now with much regret.

On seeing an anxious brooding look come over the older woman's face and wondering why Faye asked, as a diversion, if Rita wanted to hear her horoscope from the daily paper, as she usually did. *'Communication problems ease this week as extravert optimistic Jupiter travels forward through the skies, so be prepared to leave a misunderstanding in the past. But be careful with your sense of timing. Someone close to you has good fortune financially which comes with new problems,'* read Faye.

'Well, I have no idea what that means,' commented Rita.

Faye went on talking, reading now from her brochure again. *'An artist's impression of this view was used on postmarks of the 1970s with the slogan 'Captivating Colwyn Bay' ... well Richard II must have thought so. But the reason I was so fond of the hotel was that I had my wedding reception there in 1986. My husband and I loved sitting in the huge picture window with that fabulous view behind us,... it was magical.'* And on a practical note, *'It was a great place for us to start our journey to the airport for our honeymoon. The only problem was that we couldn't have a horse and carriage ride from the church up to the reception because the poor horse would never have got up that steep hill!'*

They laughed. Faye was always one to diffuse a tense situation with humour. Rita knew how bittersweet were the memories of her wedding, since Faye was a widow. Rita knew she had one son, stepchildren, cousins and an aunt, and also very dear in-laws, but no other immediate family.

Back en route they drove on down the hill through Old Colwyn and on to the promenade, sadly commenting on the state of the derelict pier and wondering what would be its fate. They stopped at a café overlooking the sea while they ate a sandwich, each contemplating their many memories of the pier in days gone by. Rita remembered the wartime concerts in which she took part, Faye remembered her school speech days in the 60s and Phil remembered some famous bands playing there in the 70s.

They were to go their separate ways now that they had arrived in town. Faye was planning to visit her Aunt, who had worked at the diamond tool factory during wartime. As well as a social visit she wanted to chat about wartime experiences to gather information for her research. She went on her way arranging to meet Rita later at a designated spot.

Rita had to say she was shocked at the difference in the town, not at all how she remembered it. *'Is it ever the same, anywhere you go, when you return?'* she thought to herself sadly. She had asked Phil to drive her around some of the areas she had known and they passed by the church hall where she had danced as a child. It was sadly derelict. She remembered the stage and a room to the side where huge wicker baskets and rails of fascinating costumes had been stored. The scent of the greasepaint which had inspired her early life had stayed in her memory and she had been mentally transported back to that particular building whenever she had encountered it, this being on many occasions.

Here she was now for real. An overwhelming sense of place and belonging filled her. They next stopped further down the road outside the house where the Joneses had lived. It was still there, one of the many semis built between the two world wars. She got out of the car and walked down the lane to the side. The coloured leaded lights in the bay window still remained in place although there had been many other alterations. The house was well kept, and now painted a cheerful shade of yellow. The lane led to a new modern housing complex. *'What if the present occupants knew of all that had gone on here? Would they want to?'* she thought as she walked back towards the car, passing an old white haired woman putting out some rubbish into her bin and she smiled towards her, and stopped suddenly shocked. She knew her. *'Excuse me, but are you Muriel? Muriel Thomas?'* They spoke as if it had been yesterday since they last met, and not over 65 years ago.

'Yes, Rita, I'm still here, in the house I moved to when I married. I didn't recognise you at first.'

'Well I wouldn't expect you to, Muriel, you wouldn't have known I was coming. I am visiting from Liverpool, and was just looking at the place where I grew up. It brings back memories.'

Muriel responded. *'Yes, I have stayed here since my husband died. It was Herbert's family home you know. I have been widowed for ten years now... You lived with the Joneses didn't you Rita? During the war.'*

'Yes, but we lost touch with them when Mary married Alf Riley and went to live in Guildford.'

They commented on further memories before exchanging details and moving on, Rita back to her waiting car and Muriel back to her house clearance. Both digesting the conversations and memories they had provoked, and wondering if they would see each other again. Rita recollected that Muriel had been a classmate of Mary, and Muriel remembered Rita as a red haired child who had gone on to achieve fame and fortune.

Rita getting back into the front seat of the car asked Phil to take her to the 'Castle Hotel'. To her utter dismay it was now closed down, boarded up and in a bad state of disrepair. An old agent's board on a pole lay trampled and rotting, unreadable in the undergrowth advertising its date of auction, but that had long passed. It appeared no one wanted the responsibility of it. Phil had warned her, but she still wanted to see for herself. They sat outside awhile while she recalled her memories of better times. Not only the days when she had danced at the concert, but also of when she visited there on holiday with her brother and his family. She used to tell the grandchildren then about her dancing there as a child in a wartime concert, and sang some of the songs to them at bedtime. She was at a loss as to what she should do then, so she then asked to be dropped off at the main street, and arranged with Phil to meet up later.

As she passed by the corner a young teenage girl was asking a rough looking bloke to help her lift her baby buggy up the steps into a pub. Could it really be this girls' own baby, she looked very young, and what would its mother think? Maybe it really *was* the girl's own baby. Rita looked at her watch, this was early in the day for anyone to be drinking, and with a baby! Here and there were empty shops, agents' signs for their sale or rent. On another corner youths passed round a cigarette, it looked home-made and she thought they must be very poor if they all had to share one between them! They saw her looking and she heard their foul language as she passed through, a strange smell permeated the air. She wafted the air with her hand. The smell was immediately replaced by another, and this caused by debris attached to the shoe of a passer-by, who suddenly realised, stopped and swore loudly and tried to scrape it off immediately on a kerb, holding a tissue to his nose with a distressed expression on his face. He didn't own a dog himself and if he did he wouldn't allow it to foul the pavement. Unfortunately this had been an on-going problem in Colwyn Bay streets. But the dog fouling and the drugs did not phase Rita, she was a feisty old woman, what would they expect, she was originally a scouser!

Walking past the old Metropole hotel she thought of the ballet classes that had taken place there in the ballroom. She paused outside remembering it fondly. A young woman was standing outside the main entrance, noticeable by her smart attire. She was exceptionally well dressed, but her clothes although seemingly of very high quality were unusual in style. Her hair was worn loose, very long, dark and silky. She seemed not to notice Rita watching her at all, and was looking down onto her lapel at a piece of gold jewellery, which looked like an old fashioned watch on a chain. Rita was amused, remembering the old style nurses watches, and immediately became intrigued by her.

This person did not seem to fit in here (she was reminded of someone, but who? Was it Faye as she may have been in her younger day? Faye did have relatives in this town. Or had she seen this woman in a dream? She couldn't quite recall where she thought she knew her from), but then she continued to study her surreptitiously, while pretending to read the menu of the restaurant next door. As the woman brushed back her long hair with her hand Rita spotted another item of jewellery, some unusual earrings, quite distinctive, and very similar to some she had owned and had recently given to Faye. They were a design of peridots set in a circle with additional stones in a different shade of green to form a lozenge shape. Rita remembered that her husband had had her own pair then made to his own design, and had given them to her years ago, it was not only diamonds he had been interested in. Peridot was said to have a tonic effect; it can heal and regenerate tissues, strengthen the metabolism and benefit the skin. It is sometimes found in meteorites. It's been mined as a gemstone for thousands of years, and is mentioned in the Bible under the name of Chrysolite. Legend says that peridot was one of the favourite gemstones of Cleopatra and that some of the 'emeralds' worn by her were actually peridots.

Having had the pleasure of them for many years and wanting to downsize her collection Rita had recently given hers to Faye because they suited her so well, echoing the colour of her green eyes. She noticed that this woman also had strikingly beautiful green eyes, bewitching. Before turning to walk away Rita remembered that like this stranger she herself probably also didn't appear to really fit in here either, although she had attempted to, and really felt she had such an affection for the town. Perhaps the mysterious woman was also a traveller, returning, reminiscing. But it was a strange coincidence about the earrings!

She felt upset, was this a relative of Faye that she hadn't told her about? And had she given away the green earrings to her *already*? Rita dismissed these wild speculations telling herself that once you give a gift then it is up to the recipient to do as they wish with it, and proceeded then along Princes Drive and Station road, stopping each time fresh memories were provoked to return to her through the constant visual triggers. She thought of a quote from Proust and surmised it applied not only to people but also places.

'Time, which changes people, does not alter the image we have retained of them.'

Since the Metropole had been converted to flats years ago where would she go for her next cup of tea? No silver jugs and white tablecloths now, she reminisced, it would be a cappuccino or a latte if she was lucky, or if not so lucky maybe in a polystyrene cup. Were there any hotels left in this town?

Llandudno she knew was still thriving as a *Queen of Resorts*, but it held no memories for her. She had dressed down as much as possible to visit what was turning out to be the '*Cinderella of seaside towns*', today she was wearing her light grey summer jacket, and she needed her comfortable shoes. There was no smart handbag to compliment her outfit, just a canvas holdall. She had a bright idea and darted into a charity shop, – of which there were many, and bought a lightweight grey mac to wear. The clouds overhead really did look ominous, and she felt more comfortable with the mac on. She took out her woollen gloves from the holdall and slipped them over her diamond ringed hands, she had been unused to wearing gloves where she usually lived.

If she had known that the town would be so disappointing she would have kept the driver on, and asked him to take her to visit the crematorium where there were inscriptions she would like to have seen, and some graves in the cemetery where she could have left some flowers, Norah's, for one, and she remembered exactly where the old lady had been buried towards the end of the war, near to the grave of Harold Lowe, the only officer on the Titanic to return in an attempt to save survivors from the icy water. She would love to visit there if only she could find a taxi, but with the rain clouds overhead the graveyard may not be the best place to be.

Rita suddenly had a brilliant idea, she would walk up to the library, yes there was something she wanted to look up She wanted to see the old back editions of the local paper. They would probably be on microfilm. She may have been mentioned in some of the concerts. She entered the red brick building and in the foyer immediately saw large photographic prints of the interior of the hotel she had just seen from the outside, portraying the sad demise of seaside holidays. She then took the lift up to the reference floor. Immediately as the door opened she saw an exhibition in the cabinet about the wartime industry in the diamond factory. There was a photograph of a former employee (was that Faye's aunt or mother-in-law?) with the son of the founder while he was visiting the town. This was of great interest to her since her own husband was connected to it, although he had not been related to the factory founder's family. She wrote her contact details in the comments book.

After searching for a while, and with the help of the very patient library staff she came up with some entries from the old newspapers, which she had been helped to print out. In April 1941 she found the entry

'Although the orchestra of thirty eight was augmented by a small number of professional players the majority were members of the Ministry of Food which is fortunate to possess this wealth of talent. The choir consisting entirely of members of the Ministry and numbered nearly one hundred.'

This was one of the many concerts she had remembered. There were other entries, which she had enjoyed browsing, some naming her. She would like to go back another day to continue searching. Perhaps Faye would help her next time. She was pleased with what she had found by herself; she could show them to her. Looking at her watch she realised it was nearly time for her to meet up again with the driver to collect Faye from her aunt's address. As she came out of the lift and approached the front door she saw that the dark thunderclouds she had seen on the horizon had reached town, and there was a heavy downpour followed by an almighty crack of lightening. It was just as well she had a little spare time to wait in the porch before making her way to Phil at the meeting point near the station, and thank goodness she had bought the mac. She had wanted to take one of the MP3 players and walk around the town with a recorded guide hearing about the history of the buildings, as she had seen advertised on a poster, but not in weather like this!

Just outside the doorway there were two young people. They were a little scruffy. She couldn't possibly know them but oddly, somehow, she felt she had an affinity for the chap, who had similar colouring to hers, or what it would have been in her younger days. He could have the Irish ancestry too, she thought. They seemed to be arguing. He struggled to pull up his hoodie, and the wet auburn hair disappeared. He had in his hand a carrier bag from an exclusive linen shop. The row became more animated and suddenly he turned on his heel and stormed off, while the girl darted into the porch where Rita was sheltering.

CHAPTER 15

Confidant

At the crematorium

Jimmy drove up the road towards the crematorium with feelings of unease and sadness, of trepidation. He was planning to look in the book of remembrance. He had had an old schoolmate, another wartime evacuee who had returned to retire to Colwyn Bay and sadly had recently died there. Jimmy had been unable to attend the funeral at the time as he had had some surgery and was told not to travel. He had felt bad about not going, but he really had not been up to it and although he had written to the family and sent a donation to the charity he now wanted to pay his respects. Trevor, the deceased, had had a good retirement although not as long as he had envisaged, Jimmy had noticed how many lived to an advanced age in this community, but Jimmy had been glad to hear that before his sudden illness Trevor had played many a game of golf and had spent time on his boat in Conwy marina.

Jimmy had by this time all but given up on the hope that he would find Liam his grandson there in the vicinity, now having explored every avenue or contact he could think of, including all the organisations and postings on websites. Now he took time out to visit the crematorium. He surmised that Liam was in some other town far away. Jimmy had no idea when he would return to this neck of the woods again so he wanted to take the opportunity to visit the book of remembrance while he could. There were many cars parked outside and it seemed that there was a service going on inside the chapel. Just one parking space was left available. He made his way to the small office where the book was kept and inquired if he could view it. He was shown towards all available books and asked staff to turn the pages to find the date he was looking for. There it was, beautifully illuminated with a touching inscription from Trevor's children and grandchildren.

'.....life is eternal and love is immortal and death just an horizon, which is the limit of our sight.' Rossiter Worthington Raymond.

There was a lot of truth in that, thought Jimmy. He briefly remembered his younger brother who had died during the war as an evacuee child taken back to Liverpool, and wondered where his grave would be. No one knew where he and their mother were buried. How he wished his mother had not taken Billy back with her, but he had wanted to go. After that the bombing had started in earnest, targeting the vital port where supplies were being brought, from America to Liverpool. He had been terrified at hearing any planes overhead returning to their base in France. Occasionally they jettisoned spare bombs, but that wasn't what terrified him, it was the thought of his relatives back in Liverpool, and his worst fears had been realised, and now he was worried about Liam. What had become of him, would they ever see him again?

His thoughts came back to Trevor and the book. He took a last look before he turned to go outside. He had seen from the threshold that a stream of mourners was emerging from the chapel now. Floral tributes had been carried to the terrace and people were bending to read the labels. He didn't expect to see anyone he knew. He had read the local paper and no one of his acquaintance had died in this town this week. But wait a minute. There was a familiar face. What was that man's name? Alf, yes, he had met him on the promenade on a previous visit here, and he was coming over this way. Well it would be rude not to acknowledge him now, wouldn't it? So they stood and chatted for a while. Alf told him that today the funeral had been for someone from church who had died, not that he had known her very well, but he felt it his duty to attend. However, he was not going to the reception at a local hotel, and had come by taxi. '*Of course I will give you a lift*' said Jimmy. Is it Rhos you want to go to? That's where I am staying and I want to pick up my bag before I make my way back to the Wirral.

They decided to have a coffee together on the promenade as the weather had cleared up. It was now a beautiful day since the lightening and deluge of rain had subsided. A rainbow could be seen over the other side of the bay towards Penmaenhead, but it looked as though it was landing on the pier. The men sat chatting again as they had when they first met. Jimmy had started to open up to Alf about his family situation since Alf had told him a few things, and they found they had some acquaintances in common, and also some mutual memories of the past, and of course a love of this town. Jimmy had been bitterly disappointed not to find his grandson, and it was an increasing cause of concern for him. It now echoed his lifelong sorrow for the loss of his brother.

After contacting the Missing Person's Help line he had become despondent. There were many posts on a local website where people were trying to trace missing relatives. Jimmy had heard that an estimated 210,000 people are reported missing in the UK each year. Most return home within seventy two hours but thousands do not. While chatting to Alf Jimmy came out with his reason for visiting the town, his search for his grandson and he even disclosed the saga of the missing diamond ring. He wouldn't normally speak so openly to a virtual stranger, but he felt vulnerable in his failure to locate Liam, and he had seemed to trust this elderly gentleman, what could be the harm in telling him, he wouldn't be repeating it to anyone they knew.

'....*Yes, they were staying at our house and my sister lost her valuable diamond ring. We assumed it was taken, because no one else had been in the house. Later we found it had got trapped inside this old music box with all the compartments. The cleaner had put it there thinking it was a jewellery box- it was either her or Liam that had to get the blame. The cleaner resigned in a huff, and Liam went on the missing list. Of course we were able to apologise to the cleaner, but Liam? We don't know where he is now.*' 'What about your sister?' asked Alf?

'*Not seen her since,*' confided Jimmy. '*We would like to get in touch you know to put things right, but she had moved abroad and left no forwarding address. I still have the ring, but me family have been split apart.*'

'*Families, eh?*' Alf gave a knowing look.

Jimmy took out a dog-eared but clear photograph out of his wallet and laid it on the table. '*This is him... Liam,*' and Alf peered at it politely before Jimmy made a move to put it away. Alf had only just put on his specs, but Jimmy doubted anyone wanted to look at it closely.

'*Just a minute, hang on there,*' said Alf, squinting, and wanting to have a closer look.

Jimmy's phone was ringing, the tone of a bell was the same popular ring tone as that on the TV show 'Deal or no deal' and reminded Alf of the old civil service phones. He didn't want Jimmy to take the call, he had news and he wanted to tell him, he *had seen* this good looking young man. That colouring was unmistakeable, with the copper-red hair, and startlingly sea-blue eyes. Yes, thought Alf, I am sure I have seen him around, more than once. But I don't know where he lives or how you could go about finding him.

Jimmy had said, '*Please excuse me, I have to take this call it's my daughter, and I am not sure that it is good news,*' and he was already flipping open the phone, '*Yes love, how's things?*' and listened for a moment – he then said a silent prayer to himself. With the good news came bad, he had taken on an ashen appearance while speaking to Maggie.

Alf was startled when he heard him say to her, '*What? Which hospital did you just say? I don't believe it. I'll get there as soon as I can love, don't worry. It will be alright. Promise you. I'll see you there,*' and snapped the phone shut. But would it be alright? The police had been in touch with her. He gathered up his photograph and his phone, dropped some money onto the table along with his business card before he fled, offering only half an explanation. '*I have to go to the hospital. Its Liam!*' *I'll be in touch, I have your number and this here is my card,*' dropping it on to the table hastily.

Alf was left to pay the bill, proffering speedy commiserations and hopes that all would be well. No full explanation had been given, was the boy in an accident? Had he taken an overdose? Alf speculated wildly, God knows there were many others in similar situations of poverty, unemployment, neglect, drug abuse... this one was fortunate, he had family looking out for him, and they were it seemed, comfortably off. (He had picked up the card and noticed the address and that it was from a firm of architects.) Everyone's child is precious to them, even when adult, the concern never grows less, and each addict is someone's son or daughter even Kayleigh, Liam, Gary and Jay.

CHAPTER 16

Fight or flight

Mid Town Colwyn Bay

Kayleigh had returned to her flat – or rather Gary's flat. She wanted to head off Liam but he had turned off his phone, why now at a time like this- she needed to warn him. *'Come on Liam, answer it.'* He couldn't be without credit, he had just had a win. What would she say to him, to Gary – or to Liam? What would she say to either of them? Just as her day was turning out great, with the win, and she was able to score off Jay on credit, and now this. She felt in her pocket for a package from Jay. She had heard it said that money doesn't solve everything, and she was at last beginning to grasp the meaning of that adage.

What lousy timing. Gary would be on the train now, how long would that give her? Why hadn't he texted her to warn her? Perhaps he wanted to surprise her; her blood ran cold as she thought of Liam getting there before her. She would be surprising him, but not in a good way. She walked up the main road towards the flat searching for Liam to warn him not to go straight to the flat.

Eventually she found him with a posh looking carrier bag. She made towards him waving the phone saying, *'What yer playing at? I've been calling yer.'* The rain had suddenly started in earnest, then thunder, and lightening lit up the sky in electric blue zig zag blasts. They had to shout to make themselves heard. He put up his hood, but her hair stuck to her forehead and the plastic clip held up her soggy wet ponytail. They rowed like they had never done so before. Money was involved. He showed her the bag with satin sheets, not listening when she said she had something important to tell him, but her priority was with the package she deeply grasped in her jacket pocket. They were conscious that an old lady in a grey coat was watching them from the doorway of the library. It was tricky, she demanded cash now, but Liam would not give Kayleigh money, he argued with her about buying drugs, he had other priorities and thought they could perhaps improve their situations. Suddenly he impetuously turned on his heel and walked off, although she called after him in vain, she couldn't catch him and her voice was drowned out in the howling wind. She called after him to come back, she had something very important to tell him, but her voice was carried away by the wind and driving rain.

* * *

Kayleigh could not think straight in her drug addled mind, she should never have had that drink with Jay. But she now knew Gary was on the way back, and that was what she had to tell Liam. They went separate ways, issues unresolved. She suspected he had cashed the money they had won. That's what they had rowed about. She was sorry now, she knew he would be fair and would have given her a half share. But who cares about money now. Why oh why hadn't she made sure she told him about Gary returning before he stormed off. She had tried to catch him and was trying to put it tactfully, waiting for the right moment, then her chance was gone because she had wasted time arguing about money. How had it come to this?

Once he got away from her Liam wondered what to do. He walked around the block and down to the promenade, sat in a shelter for a while, cooled down, then decided, '*This is stupid, he always intended to give her her share, he would go to the flat, explain and pack his bag.*' He turned and left. Had he made his way back to the flat?

Kayleigh had run to the library doorway where the old lady had been standing watching them. Too late to shelter from the rain, she was already soaked. She needed to think, time she didn't have, but she knew she had to get back to the house before Liam met Gary there. She looked at the old woman who seemed to want to speak to her. '*Your boyfriend's hair,*' said Rita, pointing in the direction in which he had fled.

'*Yeah, what about it?*' said Kayleigh nastily. '*I know he has a temper, but so have I. So would you have, if you only knew what's going on.*'

'*Yes, dear,*' said Rita. '*But I had hair that colour once, long ago before it went white. You see it runs in our family.*' The thunder cracked again loudly as if impending doom. Kayleigh had hysterics, she had to get away from the woman. She swore and made a dash towards home, it was Gary's home. She could maybe get there before Liam, even before Gary, with any luck, and she would keep trying Liam's mobile. I am so stupid, she thought to herself, why didn't I tell him?

Kayleigh was out of breath, unfit, a smoker, she was soaked to the skin and racked with coughing in the damp weather. As she turned the corner of the street she could see the light on a minicab, and saw Gary getting out of it ! She swore and steeled herself. She had never thought of herself as a good actress, or even a very good liar, despite having practised somewhat. What lies could she think of to tell? Would Jay have told Gary about Liam? She couldn't deny it, Liam's gear was all over the flat, even his underwear hanging up over the bath. Would she be able to remove it before he went in there? If only they had known Gary would get early release, and knowing him as she did it was unexpected. She tried to look pleased to see him, and smiled weakly. Could she say Liam was her brother? She had never told Gary she had a brother before, in fact she didn't have one, not that she knew of and certainly not one with red hair. What would Liam think about being called her brother?

'*Oh Gary,*' she flung her arms around him, dramatically, grimacing over his shoulder and looking to see if Liam was yet on the horizon. This was painful. '*Gary why didn't you tell me you were coming?*' and facetiously, '*I would have baked a f****** cake?*' Was Liam about to turn the corner on to the street?

Gary said, '*Let's not discuss this out here on the street. I believe Jay has given you a little something, and he told me you have had a bit of luck recently.*' They went indoors. That was not all Gary knew.

After a short interval shouting was heard to come from the flat, then a crash, and it went quiet. They were obviously having a row because of course Jay had told Gary about Liam and about the scratch card win. But Kayleigh didn't have the money yet, and Gary was determined to find out where it was. While they were waiting for Liam to arrive Kayleigh prayed that Liam wouldn't come, and she shared with Gary the drugs she had just scored from Jay... a diversion. How else could she stall for time while she worked out what to do. She knew Gary would be expecting sex, and lots of it. But he was brooding, more angry than randy, and thought, *Time enough for that later.*

Across the road Fred had been waiting for the rain to stop and was now unloading some furniture from his nearby truck. He couldn't manage this alone, not at his age, well a younger man couldn't do it alone either. He was waiting for one of his employees to arrive on the scene. He thought about going across to ask that young red haired chap to help him, he seemed pleasant enough, and was obviously out of work judging by the hours he kept. Fred stopped and scratched his head, pensively. The other guy who had just got out of the cab? He used to live there too. Not that he knew anything about the tenants in that block across the road. He just wanted a lift with his furniture from the truck. *'God knows what's going on there,'* he thought to himself. Next thing, the other bloke comes round the corner, the red haired one. *'Oi, 'scuse me mate, I need an 'and... I said can you give me a lift with this for a minute?'* he called over. He had always passed the time of day with the chap before, but today he just stormed off! Liam was in no mood for pleasantries. He glared at the man before entering the outer porch fumbling in his pocket for the key ring. Then Liam's key was heard turning in the lock. He had come to pack his bag, explain about giving her half the money not knowing that Gary was due to arrive. He found out too late. Gary heard his key turn in the door.

Kayleigh had swooned away, having not known which way to handle the situation with Gary, she had opted out of the nightmare by her use of drugs, but her avoidance would cause her to awake into a worse nightmare. While Gary waited for Liam she had overdosed. They had rowed ferociously and he would not let her past to go outside. She had to stay and suffer the consequences; she couldn't face what might happen to Liam. Gary and Liam had fought, Gary jumping in without hearing any explanation, he had heard enough from Jay. It had been a total shock for Liam to find anyone else in the flat. He had not been forewarned about Gary's release and he was taken unaware, not that he was a fighter anyway, he was way out of his depth. He had been very badly hurt. The neighbour Fred across the road had called the police, after crashing and shouting had been heard inside. That landlord of that flat was a mate of Fred's, they looked out for each other, meanwhile Fred's furniture still remained on the truck, under a tarpaulin for the rest of the day while he helped police with their enquiries.

As Fred later related to the landlord, '*The ambulance had come screaming to a halt with the siren going. Liam and Kayleigh were taken to hospital while the Police arrested Gary again for GBH!*' He had been released for less than five hours.

Kayleigh had been in a bad way when the ambulance arrived and it had been touch and go, a fact which shocked Liam when he heard it after he came round in the hospital. The ambulance crew and triage team had searched his clothing for information to find out who was his next of kin. They didn't find a large amount of cash, as he had been unable to cash the money from the scratch card win that day, and so had extended his overdraft in order to buy her the satin sheets. She hadn't believed him. They found his mobile but without the ICE number they needed. Kayleigh wouldn't have known, and she was in a coma anyway, who was her ICE? '*In Case of Emergency?*' No one knew, but Liam's driving licence from his wallet identified him, it was still registered to his parents' address, their number was found and they were notified.

As Maggie and her husband flew into their car to start the journey from Hoylake, she grabbed her mobile phone and called her father Jimmy, who she knew was after all looking in the right vicinity and he was on hand to arrive at casualty before Maggie. Jimmy was put *in loco parentis* having driven the shorter distance from the café after being at the crematorium.

Liam had narrowly escaped death by violence and it seemed he had no permanent damage. As for his family, all was forgiven. This was a way for Liam to be reconciled with his grandfather Jimmy, in what he thought was an irredeemable situation, having fallen out with parents. He was ashamed he had stolen money from them for drugs, and while he understood that they would be angry about that, he was indignant that he should be blamed for taking the valuable diamond ring of Rita's. No way did he want to be blamed for something he hadn't done, he wanted to hang on to that shred of self-respect.

However, he was glad when Jimmy eventually explained how the ring had been found. What a fuss, when it had been in the music box all along, maybe put there by the cleaner, as this box looked similar to a jewellery box Rita had – with inlaid wood. So no one got the blame. Sadly Rita still didn't know that. She had cut herself off from the family.

CHAPTER 17

Liam's Turning Point

Heaven?

Liam felt he was in a good place, all was well. He had woken gently, feeling a light touch on his wrist and a glowing aura all around him. Slowly opening his eyes he immediately wondered if had died and gone to heaven, because in front of him was the most beautiful girl he had ever seen, the most lovely, a vision of loveliness. He had heard about love at first sight, now he knew it could really happen and he was experiencing it. He thought it worth suffering all he had been subjected to, getting beaten up as well as months of feeling out on a limb, just to meet her. The 'angel' was wearing a nurses uniform, and a genuinely divine smile with her perfectly pearl-like teeth and compassion in her warm dark eyes.

There was the clue in the uniform, he looked around him to see a range of medical equipment and curtains around his bed. He could imagine the 'angel' wearing a wedding dress. He tried to speak, and when he tried to shift position he noticed the drip leading to the needle in the back of his hand and realised with a shock why he was there. The events of the last few days came flooding back to him in a blur and a panic, wondering how Kayleigh was. *'Easy there,'* she said, *'don't move now, we've all been in bit worried about you.'*

He smiled back at her with eyes the colour of the sea in the Bay of Colwyn on a good day, and tried to speak, noticing the absence of a few of his own teeth, the small movement left him feeling distinctly woozy. *'What's your name?'*

'Grace,' she answered.

'Oh Grace, you suit that name, and what's your phone number?' said Liam. She knew then he must be feeling better.

When Liam was out of danger and the visitors sat around the bed Jimmy and the family eventually discussed the old problem about the reason why they had been out of touch, and the lost ring. It had up to this point been the *'elephant in the room'* It had been the reason why he left the area and disappeared. All was resolved, being of little importance in the scheme of things. Then Liam showed his grandfather the mobile phone picture of the interior of the Castle Hotel. There were tears all round. Liam had survived a vicious attack, but despite the reconciliation with his family he suffered depression and guilt about his girlfriend, Kayleigh, in hospital. At first he was not well enough or mobile enough to visit her in the ward. He had a lot of time to think about his future and to plan the turnabout in his life. He succeeded somehow.

After a fortnight the doctors were pleased with his progress. His friendship with nurse Grace had blossomed. It had contributed greatly to his good recovery. It seemed she also had feelings for him too, although she had not expected, or had actively promised herself not to have any relationships with patients and had always succeeded in this until now. But she also knew he had a girlfriend in another ward and asked him if he was feeling up to visiting her.

'The physio thinks you ought to get a bit of practice in with your crutches. Do you think you are up to going to see Miss Kelly on ward 11?' Grace had checked out Kayleigh's condition and liaised with

other staff members who had ensured that this was appropriate or advisable, but also she was interested to know where she stood with Liam. She was a professional and had as yet no involvement with him or any other patient. She did like him, but perhaps he was just a flirt, and gave all women this much attention. '*Miss Kelly*, Kayleigh, *she is out of danger now you know*'.

'*I have been thinking about that,*' said Liam. '*I do have some unfinished business with her.*' Of course he had the money from the win in his account and he wanted her to have it. His family had visited constantly all week. The nightstand next to his bed was a mass of flowers, fruit and get well cards. He wondered if she had had any visitors.

The next day, after some serious thought and soul searching he hobbled over to the women's ward, taking with him one of the boxes of chocolates he had been given and some of the flowers. He chose a basket arranged with brightly coloured gerbera. The accompanying nurse carried it for him. When he arrived at Kayleigh's bedside he was shocked at the state in which he found her. She had the privacy of her own room not only because of the seriousness of her condition, but also because she was on suicide watch, and also faced criminal charges. She had been caught trying to get her hands on cleaning fluids to drink them. (She had remembered reading about Billy Joel having drunk furniture polish at one time, a low point of his life).

Liam was warned not to be there too long. She wasn't up to a long visit and he was relieved he was not expected to sit with her for any length of time; it could be awkward after all the police interviews and so on. He had just wanted some sort of closure on their relatively short-lived relationship. There she was, looking very small, pale and fragile in the bed, her face as white as the pillowcase, devoid of any kind of make up or fake tan, and her hair washed and straight down on to her shoulders. He thought she actually looked quite sweet, more innocent. However, he remembered what had happened that day and asked if she felt up to talking about it.

'*I am so glad you have come to see me Liam. Thank you. I wanted to apologise for what happened to you,*' she was full of remorse. '*I should have told you we were expecting Gary back at the flat. But I had just found out meself and I was trying to find a way...*'. Her lip then started to tremble. She seemed to have had a personality change, she didn't seem like the Kayleigh he had known.

He helped her out. '*Well I didn't exactly give you a chance did I? I stormed off in the rain. But there is something I want to talk to you about. About what we were arguing about that day...the money. I'll hand over what's left to you. I mean all that's left. I had to put it in the bank for safety that day. Most of it is still there – except what went on my overdraft.*'

'*But what about you, you will need some money when you leave here?*'

'*I am going to stay with my family on the Wirral. They will support me. That's the other thing I wanted to tell you. My Granddad was in town that day and he came straight here. He had spent quite a lot of time looking for me actually,*' she looked surprised. And he went on to reassure her, '*But we'll keep in touch, yeah?*'

Kayleigh then admitted that she would have to go to court for various offences which had caught up with her. If she was acquitted would she be able to stay in the flat in town? But she was ready to plead guilty to all charges. Of course Gary was back inside for the foreseeable future.

'*Liam, when I can, I am going to relocate to Manchester to be near me gran. She has been ill for some time and she is not getting any better. Please don't worry about me. Please feel free to go where you will be looked after.*'

Liam breathed a sigh of relief. Their arrangement was mutually amicable.

Kayleigh had pulled through after remaining unconscious for some time. She then faced a criminal conviction for possession of class A drugs, soliciting, shoplifting, benefit fraud. The list was long. These were not first offences, therefore she would be sent down after her recovery. At first it had been touch and go whether she would live. Ambulance staff had searched in Kayleigh's oversized purse and found a card with next of kin – a grandmother in Manchester's Moss side. This was the lady who had brought her up. Sadie Kelly, born in 1924. Her daughter, (Kayleigh's mother) was Suzie Kelly born 1956 when Sadie was 32. Suzie had gone abroad as soon as Kayleigh was born in the early '80s, abandoning her new-born daughter Kayleigh with the grandmother. Sadie had brought up the baby as best she could, she was even the one who had named her, not after the aviator, but after a pub of the same name with different spelling Cayley. But by now Sadie was too ill and infirm to travel or to do anything for Kayleigh, She lived in a care home was suffering with Alzheimer's.

Liam had ambitious plans to turn his life around, to become a youth worker, an advisor, to help others who had been in his situation. He wanted to put something back, and to build up some esteem, to feel worthy enough to deserve Grace. He came to see a different side of life, and mixed in different circles, in a community, as an alternative to the underclass to which he had sadly belonged temporarily while away from his family. Big changes were ahead for him, his life now had a new perspective.

CHAPTER 18

Reconciliation

Spain

Rita and Faye hadn't returned to Spain until early September. They had spent the rest of their trip visiting friends in the Lake District, enjoying the peace, breath-taking scenery and coolness of climate. They had also enjoyed a number of National Trust properties, and especially those among the beauty of the tranquil lakes. They had hired a car and Faye had driven, returning to Liverpool in time to visit Hetty in the nursing home after her surgery. She had made a good recovery, and Rita was relieved to hear it. They also visited friends and relatives of Faye's, since Faye generously shared her extended family of cousins and in-laws with Rita. Rita had tentatively asked questions about the mysterious woman she had seen, who looked like Faye and was wearing the green peridot earrings but Faye knew nothing about it. She still had hers and wore them to show Rita. *'Hey Rita, you didn't think I had pawned them did you?'* she had joked. Rita had to put it down to coincidence, but she now regretted not speaking to the woman. Hindsight had never been an exact science.

It wasn't until she had been back in Spain for several days that Rita started to reflect on the disappointment she had experienced in Wales. She realised that a town, its architecture or landscape is not enough, although it provokes the memories. *'Time, which changes people, does not alter the image we have retained of them.'* Marcel Proust had said. What she wanted was to be in touch with the people. Who would be left? Where were they all? And how had they changed? She had reached a contemplative state of mind.

Liam wasn't the only member of his family to turn over an idealistic leaf. Philanthropy, the effort or inclination to increase the well-being of humankind was high on Rita's list of priorities as she advanced in age. She had a solicitor's appointment to rewrite her will – and had contemplated endlessly what she would do with her fortune. Some would go to medial research, and other favourite charities. Some would go to family, regardless of the family rift, so Liam and his sisters would benefit, and the sisters also had children to consider. She also wanted to contribute to the regeneration of Colwyn Bay, not just the structural repair and renewal but for the education of young people who want to pursue in particular a theatrical career, as she had. She would not forget Faye's Heritage projects for Oral History. Rita was so super wealthy, and planned wisely, but she also wanted to spend some of it now on a lavish party.

Rita, Faye and Lorenz Crozier, a Swiss solicitor sat outside among the bougainvillea and hibiscus. Lorenz had flown in from Geneva that same day. He and Rita had had a long association, he had always acted on her husband's behalf in legal matters, so he was someone she trusted implicitly. He wore a lightweight cream suit with a pale blue shirt, and felt the heat in the Spanish September sun, although he was not as formally dressed as he was accustomed to being. He mopped his brow as he shuffled through a sheaf of paperwork. Faye poured him a glass of sangria over ice.

'Yes, Madame Van Royen,' said Lorenz. *'Please, call me Rita,*

Lorenz, we've known each other long enough now, how many years? We don't have to stand on ceremony.'

'Very well, er... Rita, this is a list of your assets,' he was quite frankly overawed by her. She was so super rich, who would ever know from appearances, she was so unassuming, but she had values. These so called 'celebrities' of today would be put right in the shade in comparison, if they only knew. Shade! That is something he would value at this minute. He was in awe of her for two reasons, she having been a superstar, and the Van Royen's being one of his wealthiest clients.

He wished they had chosen to sit indoors in the air conditioning instead of on the ballustraded terrace. He passed Rita several sheets of paper in a folder, commenting. *'You will see that the first page is your portfolio of properties.'* She perched her Chanel varifocals on her nose and perused the list. *'Oh look, Faye, we still have those properties in Liverpool.'*

Faye wondered why she said 'we'. *'Same tenants after all these years.'* She had not taken a close interest in her property portfolio since her husband had died. Time now to sharpen up.

'Lorenz. I am ready to let the house in Belgium go now; it has been empty for long enough.' This had been the home she had had with her late husband, a country mansion with a considerable area of land surrounding it. It had been closed up and heavily alarmed, with security guards posted since it was full of very valuable contents. Caretakers lived in a cottage in the grounds. *'I will go over to visit with Faye to see what is to be kept and what should be sold, if that's alright with you Faye?'*

Faye looked at her in amazement. *'Yes of course Rita.'* Faye had as yet never been there.

'And the house in Florida?' queried Lorenz.

'Yes let's sell that too. I don't want to go there any more.' Rita was ready to move on with her life. Faye's eyes widened.

'And your house in Switzerland?' said Lorenz. 'Your husband hoped you would retire there together one day. I also have a list of the charities he favoured.'

There were shares in a diamond mine in Brazil, as well as all the diamonds and gold in vaults, all inherited from her husband. The rest of the sheets itemised the multiple stocks and bonds in her portfolio which came to many tens of millions of pounds, there were royalties from films, music and books. There were valuable classic cars at all the properties, her husband had been a collector, and they had lain under dustsheets in vast garages for years. Rita was ready to consolidate her assets. No one would have believed that the old lady in the grey mac walking around Colwyn Bay would have such a net worth. If only they had known!

She had her favourite charities to remember, some of them worthy causes in Belgium, but it was Colwyn Bay where she wanted to make the greatest difference. She did not forget her family and intended to help every last one of her relatives, it was a relief for her to get these plans in place. They would take Lorenz to one of the coastal restaurants after this was cleared up, and all details could be finalised later once she had signed the necessary papers. Lorenz could go back to his hotel to freshen up first; he looked somewhat hot and bothered.

Rita was glad to have the copies of the local newspaper forwarded to her, from Liverpool and North Wales. They were also able to get hold of a few back editions – so they could catch up, and Faye was good at bringing up pages on the internet. One newspaper had arrived that morning and now that Lorenz had left them for a break before dinner she looked forward to reading it. However when she got down to it she was dismayed at the reports of crime and poverty. She had had a taste of the decline on her recent visit, she would not forget. Her contribution to regeneration would start immediately, why wait for her will, especially after what she had discussed with her accountant. This was something else Lorenz could deal with for her, she turned the page of the newspaper and an article caught her eye.

'*Grandfather and Grandson reunited after vicious attack.*' The young man was pictured in hospital with the older man by his bedside, and she went on to read the story.

William Johnson, of no fixed address, suffered an unprovoked attack from Gary Wilson of Plas Central apartment building after Johnson had a win from a scratch card. Also injured in the attack was Ms Kayleigh Kelly of the same address. Both have been hospitalised in a serious condition and were unable to comment. Mr Fred Daniels of Daniels Furniture store called the police after he heard a disturbance from the ground floor apartment at the front of the house of multiple occupation. Mr Wilson had recently been released from serving a prison sentence and is now on remand on a further charge of GBH. Mr Daniels commented ' I think I called the police at exactly the right time, I knew when I saw that chair come through the window that there was something seriously wrong going on in there. I 'm glad I did call. I would not like to have crossed Mr Wilson, but I was surprised to see him back in prison so soon...

Rita was shocked to see such a sensational news story, and immediately looked for the date on this paper, and soon found it... August 21st. It had taken a while to arrive to her in Spain. She had actually been in the town on that very day, and had then returned to Liverpool to embark on her tour of the Lakes. It was that day of the terrible thunderstorm when she'd sheltered outside the library. She didn't know where Plas Central apartments were. She went on reading.

William Johnson is pictured here with his grandfather James Gerard from Hoylake. Maggie Johnson, William Johnson's mother said, how fortunate it was that her father, Mr Gerard had been in the area when they heard the news that William, known as Liam, had been attacked and was in hospital. He was able to come straight to the hospital. Liam had been away from home for some time and they had not recently been in touch.'

Maggie, a private sort of person, had later regretted speaking to the journalists, and showing them the picture she carried with her, but she was so stressed and relieved that Liam was going to be alright, and pull through after his injuries and on a natural high, that she hadn't thought straight. She had had little experience with journalists.

But Rita was flabbergasted to read an editorial write up about Liam Johnson. This was a story about her great nephew and his family from the Wirral, and how they raced to his bedside. She actually felt guilt at being out of touch for so long. It wasn't until later that she recalled seeing a boy with copper coloured hair outside the library in the rain. But how could they have recognised each other after so long, and both out of context?

Immediately she fetched her writing pad. She didn't want to phone, after such a long silence, but wanted to say how she felt, to give her support, and to see how the offer would be received. She had no e mail address for him and had never reached her brother by phone and hadn't realised he had been away during her visit. She wrote the letter in a flourishing hand

> *Dear Jimmy,*
> *You will be surprised to hear from me after all these years. I have been living in Spain. I hope you are at the same address and that this will reach you. I am writing because have read about you in the local paper, which I had sent to me here, and I just wanted to express my concern and say*

that I hope Liam is alright after his injuries. Please do let me know.

You will not believe it but I was in Colwyn Bay that day, of all days. I thought about you a lot as I have frequently over the years. I spent a lot of time thinking of how we grew up there as evacuees, and also about when we used to return with your children and grandchildren. The Castle Hotel, our favourite haunt, with the murals, is closed down I see. What will become of it?

I tried to call you when I was recently in Liverpool, but there was never an answer. It has been a good few years since we met and I am sorry we have not made it up with you about the row we had. Perhaps we can put our differences aside now. It really doesn't matter a damn about the ring. I have others. Jimmy I am so sorry I made a fuss, it was the principle really. I wish Liam well and hope he makes a full recovery. I hope the rest of the family are well, I send my love to you all.

Your sister Rita.

She re read it through once then sticking down the envelope before she changed her mind she called Faye to tell her what she had seen and to ask her to post the letter special delivery, and proceeded to explain all about it.

The letter was delivered within days

Saturday

The excitement had almost died down with the family in Hoylake, Just as Jimmy was thinking things were more or less back to normal, after all the driving down the A55 constantly back and forth to visit the hospital. The post dropped on the mat with a thud. Jimmy walked down the hallway towards the ornate glass porch door to gather it up. Nothing exciting he thought, the gas bill, council tax and a bank statement, the usual collection of colourful junk mail, then he noticed a letter from abroad. His curiosity was getting the better of him as he ripped it open before he reached the kitchen and turning over the page of cream vellum he looked first to see the signature on the bottom. He was incredulous ...Spain...all these years...that's where she had been that sister of his ! And he had read the letter almost in disbelief. He was alone in the house, his wife had just left in the car to go to their daughter Maggie's house, where Liam was now ensconced, being thoroughly spoiled after his ordeal. Although Jimmy had to admit, he seemed to have changed a lot. It had obviously made him grow up somewhat. He was talking about returning to the Bay to see that nurse he had met in the hospital. Alone in the house Jimmy had no one to tell about this incredible piece of news. Without delay he grabbed the phone and dialled the number on the top of the expensive and luxurious stationery.

At this time Rita was relaxing on her patio with Faye. Lorenz had gone back to Switzerland to draw up legal papers. The two women were talking and reminiscing about their trip, drinking 'mocktails' of exotic fruit mixes, gazing at the view on the coast out ahead over the landscape where they could see ships on the horizon, wondering whether they should take a cruise. The phone rang a few times before Rita said, *'Faye would you mind fetching the phone out here for me please?'*

Faye quickly darted inside and returned with a worried expression and handed Rita the phone, saying, *'He says its personal.'*

The voice at the other end said, *'Can I please speak to Ms Margarita Gerard?'*

'Speaking,' she said and the answer came back, *'Rita is that you?'*

'Who is this please?'

'Rita, it's Jimmy yer brother.'

They were both close to tears, full of emotion yet feeling a surrealistic quality to the reconciliation. They managed to hold on to their voices, they had so much to say and no time to cry. Jimmy eventually explained the false accusation of Liam stealing diamond ring. It was found. There it was all the time in the old music box, which played 'Home Sweet Home', but they had been unable to tell Rita as they had lost touch. She had left her previous address, and they didn't know she was living in Spain. Rita was understandably emotional.

Jimmy, I don't care about the damn ring, I want me family back. Yes, yes I will come back over for a visit to Hoylake. When is it convenient for you?'

When she put the phone down she could no longer contain her emotions, she burst into tears and then pulling herself together said firmly, without explanation, 'Faye, *as quick as you can, please book us some flights to Liverpool to John Lennon airport, can you get first class? And a car to meet us. Get that chap Phil, the one we had before. He gave us a card didn't he? I liked him. Is Tuesday too early for us to go?'*

Faye had not expected to be visiting old haunts again so soon. Then Rita got up from her lounger and walked over to the balcony, watching the liners, which had sailed away from the port, for the first time fully realising the full meaning of the phrase 'Ships that pass in the night.' She regretted all the time she had wasted in the feud with her family. Who knows how much time is left, she intended to seize the day.

CHAPTER 19

Alf and Friends Reunited

Colwyn Bay promenade

On a warm September day Jimmy sat with Alf again at that same café. They had become friendly since their last dramatic meeting that day when Jimmy had rushed off from the cafe to Liam's bedside in hospital. Alf had looked him up from the business card which Jimmy had hastily flung down on the table when he rushed off, as he had been worried about the dramatic exit.

Since then they had kept in touch after their brief acquaintance that summer, Jimmy was filling in the gaps of the story to Alf. *'It seemed it has been a turning point for the whole family, not just Liam.'* Thinking regretfully to himself, *'The only person to complete the family now is Rita.'* They had been in touch and they were expecting her to arrive very soon. Modern music permeated the air outside the promenade kiosk and gulls rose crying on the wind, signalling imminent rain.

Alf was still enjoying talking about the war years to anyone who would listen. *'For a lot of people in the Bay the Ministry of Food did them a good turn, giving them a job throughout the war and the chance of becoming established civil servants later when examinations returned, This meant them leaving here for London and Guildford – but what jobs would there have been in the post war years? None.'*

What jobs were there in the present? For the unqualified – even for the overqualified who had huge student loans?

Jimmy did not mind hearing all this, in fact he enjoyed the conversation very much. *'You know I am so glad we have met and it is all coming back to me. So many memories and I can't say they were all bad. I had many happy days here. Of course I used to come here in the fifties, just before I got married, it was great then. I used to go to the open-air swimming pool then, they had great gala nights. My sister sometimes performed in them, just for fun. She sang.'*

'Oh, your sister? You told me about the misunderstanding. Where is she now?' inquired Alf.

'We have had a reconciliation and she is planning a visit here very soon,' said Jimmy. Whether he would have told Alf more about his family quarrels we'll never know. An amazing reunion was about to take place.

Although Alf wanted to hear more, he looked up at that moment and had to stop Jimmy to say, *'Sorry to interrupt you but here is my wife, and her friend, they have been shopping. Hello dear, we'll make room for you both.'* He turned to Jimmy to introduce him. But Jimmy was ready to introduce himself.

He stood up and offered his hand. *'Hello.'*

'Oh, I'm Jimmy,' said the interested stranger, and Alf also introduced his wife. *'This is my wife Mary, and our friend Miranda who was also evacuated here during the war. We go back a long way, Mary and Miranda were at school together here in Colwyn Bay.'*

They sat together chatting and Jimmy asked questions of Mary, a beautiful, graceful delicate eighty-something lady with champagne blonde hair, and light blue eyes, who became animated and after the brief introductions excitedly took over the conversation. *'Did Alf tell you we have been married 65 years now? We met at a dance at the pier pavilion. Then Alf joined the navy, I left school and became a ballet student in Chester and I had to travel* every day. At the time all the trains had their carriages blacked out – not very pleasant especially on the way home in the blackout. When I finished training I went to college and learned shorthand and typing.'

Jimmy asked, 'Oh, couldn't you have gone on the stage?'

Mary answered, 'I was only 17 and... well... dancing was not a reserved occupation. Anyway my mother did not want me to be away from home. But I became a dance teacher later on.'

But Jimmy wanted to know more about the war years in Colwyn Bay. 'So did you work for the Ministry as well?'

Mary answered, 'Yes, eventually, because as a shorthand typist for the Ministry of Food, then I **was** in a reserved occupation, and I could be here when Alf came home on leave from the navy.'

'Do you know when I remember about it I don't think people fully appreciated the valued contribution Colwyn Bay made to the war effort,' Jimmy commented.

Mary said, 'That's true, not just the Ministry, but in so many other ways. I didn't know at the time that there were several industries doing vital war work. Some of our troops were stationed here and of course the Americans came in their thousands straight off the troop ships. Obviously they were training in preparation for the D Day landings. I wonder what happened to them; from what we saw on the newsreels the losses were terrible. Some of our local girls were infatuated with the yanks with their smart uniforms and their smooth talk.'

'Oh yes, you mean like Sadie Kelly?' chipped in Alf.

Miranda, the other lady, with a quite different accent, wanted in on this conversation now and said, 'My family lodged at a large boarding house, as my dad was a civil servant from London. Mrs Owen was our landlady. There were some American servicemen and nurses also staying there. We found them very pleasant and only too pleased to talk about their families and the places they had come from. It was odd but one lad had signed the visitors book – German –

not surprising because I expect his family had originated in Germany.'

Mary said, *'My family took evacuees, we had to, although we didn't have a lot of room.'*

Miranda went on, *'The Australian crew of a Lancaster bomber came to the Owen' house after their mission over Germany. Olwen Owen made a fuss of them and we were all deeply distressed to hear that the pilot, Bluey, got killed on his motorbike outside his home in a remote part of Australia. This after surviving the bombings.'*

Jimmy's mind had been ticking over, some of this conversation was familiar to him and he started to realise he had a connection to these people. *'Just a minute there, can we go back a bit, did you say you had evacuees?'* He directed his question to Mary.

'Of course, everyone had to.'

'Were they the Gerards, and young Billy who returned with his mother and never survived the raid on Liverpool?'

'How do you know about that?' said Mary, shocked.

'I am Jimmy. Jimmy Gerard.'

Mary gasped, then leaped up and hugged him, feeling very emotional. *'Little Jimmy, Why did we not keep in touch?'*

Because you went to live in Guildford with Alf, when all the other civil servants were transferred. I am sorry not to have recognised you straight away Mary, but we haven't seen each other for, how many years? More than 60. And of course I have changed too, since I was twelve. Look me hair's white now!'

Mary asked, *'What happened to Rita?'*

'Well,' said Jimmy, *'now you're asking.'*

The sound of the sea, and the seagulls' cries drowned out their voices.

They had walked up through the cutting and under the railway bridge which was now a footpath while they remembered it as a road, to the town opposite where the fairground used to be, and searched for a café to sit and have a chat over a cup of tea.

'Oh there are so many stories,' said Alf to Jimmy, 'and I wrapped it in the paper and put it in my pocket, so when I came out of the cinema I looked at it and she had only given me the lipstick instead. It was wrapped up just like a sweet you see because all the metal had been used for the war, they couldn't afford metal for lipstick cases, and that lipstick in the paper had got into the bag of sweets by mistake.'

Miranda hoped he would accept her repeated apology, as late as it was. 'Oh I am so sorry Alf, I don't know how it got into there.'

And Mary commented, 'Oh Alf, it didn't do you any harm did it?'

'Well no, except that I had pink teeth'.

'Shimmering heartbreak pink!' giggled Mary.

Alf went on. 'I lived to tell the tale. In fact my mother always said – worse things happen at sea.'

And Mary said, 'Well you **would** know that, being on that minesweeper in the channel.'

CHAPTER 20

2013 'When You Return'

"You must be the change you wish to see in the world"
                                                    Gandhi.

Preparations were underway for a party. There had been difficulty finding a suitable venue, but since the position of the restoration of the pier was still in dispute – that would have been their number one choice had it been available. But they booked the Cricket Club pavilion for the dinner. This was a reunion for the friends of Rita's *Foundation*, a charity she had started up. It had given her a new lease of life. A branch of it was called 'When you return' on a theme of reuniting estranged family members or missing persons.

She was by now nearly eighty four and had been regularly visiting her brother Jimmy, sister-in-law Maggie and family, and had spent much more time in Colwyn Bay. In fact she had bought an apartment in the town. Not one of those purpose built, but part of an old characterful Victorian house, which had been under threat of demolition, but which she had overseen a sympathetic and tasteful renovation and refurbishment. After seeing that this was not only possible but successful, others had followed suit and she had started a trend. She was very comfortable there but kept her home in Spain for *rainy days* and the worst weather, and her family from the Wirral had an extended invitation to visit there. She was happy to be back living in the town she remembered as her girlhood home. She knew she was in a privileged position, but she had worked hard for a great deal of her riches, and now she intended to put in place plans to share and utilize them.

No one had any idea she was so wealthy (not even Rita herself it seemed, she had never been motivated by money), and her family loved her for herself, and for all the years they had been together, despite the relatively short gap when she was distanced from them. Even when she had been away working she was always on the end of the telephone. Blood was evidently thicker than water, after all.

She bitterly regretted the rift with her family in the past, which had cost them all years of wasted time and lack of contact. It was not only Liam who had been a missing person. To make amends she had thought about buying a business in town anonymously and getting Liam in as manager, but she knew he was proud and may have his own ideas about what he wanted to invest his time in. She had heard all was going well for him, having made a good recovery and still seeing the nurse he had met in the hospital. She had made sure she had been in touch She wanted to hold a dinner for her charity launch, and also invite so many supporters and old friends, as many as she could find.

She had known Grace's grandmother, Muriel in the war years from the concerts, and Muriel had been at school with Mary and Miranda. Muriel was several years older than she was. Liam and Grace were unsure whether to go into business, because they were happy in their caring roles, Grace as a nurse, working on a drug rehabilitation programme now, and Liam was training as a youth worker, work he found rewarding and for which he had developed a passion. Their strong commitment to their vocation meant she would have had to find someone else to run the business for her. As Liam had said, '*What about those who don't have an aunt to do that for them?*' He was not bitter about the mistake that had accused him of theft years ago, but he knew that he had deserved to have the finger of suspicion pointed at him. His life had turned around since he had met Grace. They were to be married and were keen to start a family.

On the evening of the party waiters hovered, wearing black waistcoats and long French aprons, they were busy polishing glasses and cutlery to a high shine. The tables were set with stylish floral displays. The music of decades ago, at Rita's request, played on the sound system, giving ambiance, reviving memories.

As many old friends as possible had been located. A diamantiere from Belgium, Hans Wins had come with his wife, Suzanne, since Rita had written in the comment book in the library after seeing the exhibition , back in 2009 they had struck up a friendship. Hans was the son of the founder of the diamond factory and had known Rita's late husband when they were boy scouts. All guests were mingling. Hetty Barnstaple was there talking to an old school friend of Rita's. They were discussing the wartime and the old school two tier system, as well as air raids, concerts and Shirley, a friend from Cumbria asked, '*What was your stage name Mrs Barnstaple?*' A friend of Faye's Ella was there; she had an involvement and input to the charity with art therapy, and was a consultant. She was a well-known artist and had her own residential art school 'The Dragon School' in the Welsh hills. She and Faye had been at school together. Faye was very excitedly telling people that her stepson now had a baby, a boy called Ethan and his middle name was to be that of his grandfather. Also her own son was engaged to be married.

Two other old friends had just met up unexpectedly at the bar. Alf and Harry were both local men, whose wives also knew each other, and were also chatting animatedly together. Alf said to his friend, Harry, '*I wonder if it was a good idea to get us together after all these years. Rather a special occasion when we are all in our late eighties. It is surprising to see how many of us there are with not a lot of us on zimmer frames!*'

Harry answered, '*It was rather a poignant notice in the local paper, about the charity and about reuniting – it caught my attention right away and I wondered.... Yes I thought, I wonder if many of my old pals are still around. It's ridiculous but you know friends lose touch when they leave school and go out to work – they just don't make the effort, and especially if they leave the area.*'

'*Yes I agree,*' said Alf, '*but in our case with the war and the disruption and I confess I have even forgotten the names of some of my friends. Of course some did not survive the war – my best pal Paul was killed in a flying accident and Ray was a casualty in Greece. There were several others if I can think of them. If I get the chance I would like to talk to each one – what did they do when they left school? College, degrees, work and of course war service – so many questions unanswered.*'

Alf paused a while and sipped his beer thoughtfully, then asked Harry. '*Did you know that someone is writing an account of Colwyn Bay during the war years? She and her friends are having a reunion this year. Her name is Faye, she is here tonight, and she lived here herself as a girl. She is writing about the vital contributions made to the war effort? I found it difficult to believe that much happened here, and what on earth did people do in this quiet seaside town to merit any recognition, especially when we in the services were risking our lives in Germany, Italy and the Far East?*

'*Well,*' said Harry, '*There were also many other contributions in other parts of North Wales like art from the National Gallery and*

Hampton Court hidden in the slate mines, the designing and building of Mulberry harbour in Conway, and there was the diamond tool industry at the factory here and prolific assembly of jeeps at the garage.'

Alf continued with his train of thought that people didn't realise that so much happened during wartime when servicemen were away fighting, that truth was paralleled in every area. *'That was a view held by many until they stopped to give some thought to all that happened here between 1939 and 1945. I haven't time to spell it out and will leave it for a time when we can sit down over a drink – it is a story worth telling. Good luck to Faye. I for one am proud of Colwyn Bay – it has suffered so much and continues to be a very special place to me, although, it does deserve the regeneration now. I read Lord Woolton's memoirs, they were written back in 1956. Do you know he never mentioned this town. You can understand the need for secrecy at the time, but now after all this time no one talks about it or even remembers it, and yet there are still a lot of people here, and all over the country who can tell you more about it, that is if anyone is interested.'*

Harry agreed that the work of the headquarters of the Ministry of Food was unaccredited. They discussed a poem written by a former Ministry employee, June Lee. In fact she had been recruited to address envelopes when she was thirteen in the holidays from County School, but had gone on to have a long career as a legal secretary, retiring at 67. She had felt her education had been seriously disrupted by the war and the many evacuees overcrowding her school. The poem commented on the difference technology had made to her profession and she had called it 'The Secretary's Lament'.

It does not seem so long ago, and yet it's tens of years
Since I first entered Lawyers' realm, a youngster full of fears.

There seemed so much you have to learn life took a new
    dimension, The rules were strict, the leeway small
And clients you did not mention.
The work was hard and constant; you tried with all your
    might.
You then went off to lessons when you finished work at night.
The ultimate was seen to be shorthand and typing skills
    for those with secretarial flair with never any frills.
Admiration filled you as your seniors showed the way
One day maybe you'd join their ranks though that seemed far
    away
Looking back, I made it ...and did reach the dizzy heights
Good shorthand and fingers that covered keys in flights.
Then came the revolution, which had sent so many reeling
What happened to the dignity, the caring and the feeling.
Maybe as we worked on in cloistered same routine
We did not know the 'art' was dead. Long live the 'new
    machine'.
Now there comes an echo from the far and distant past
I can sense the heartache when the first machines were cast
All the dedication and the beauty of the quill
Esteem we humbly offer to that discipline and skill.

    Harry's sister had also worked for the Ministry of Food.
'That's the problem with food,' he said, *'it's only important when
you're hungry, afterwards people forget. What if there hadn't been
any food during the war? What if this area had been bombed too?
After all Lord Haw Haw knew about the Ministry being here. We used
to hear him say so in his broadcasts, although more popular
entertainment programmes were planned to be on at the same time.
Doesn't bear thinking about, what would have happened if the
Ministry had been targeted. Shall we move over to our table? I am*

hungry now when I think of times when there was a lack of food.'

Alf was hungry too, but had to answer before they made their way to their table. *'I've written my story down. Had a book published about my experiences on a minesweeper in the channel. And I sent my memories of the town in wartime to the Imperial War Museum. They are there for anyone who wants to read them. My grandson says he wishes more people would write down their memories. Come let's see who will be at our table, and where they have been these past 68 years.'*

The sun was just going down behind the Little Orme across the cricket field. In the golden evening light, Rita, resplendent and elegant in her pale designer chiffon, with many diamonds sparkling at her throat, sat at the head of the top table. She had told Faye she had felt sixty tonight, not in her eighties. During the meal she found an appropriate moment to tap her glass with her fork, it chimed to signify that she wanted to say a few words. Her family were all here, Yes really, *all* of them. Jimmy her brother, his wife and daughter with their children including of course Liam, Jimmy's grandson and Liam's fiancée Grace, was wearing the huge diamond ring Rita had given them with her blessing, and Faye was wearing the green peridot earrings which always accentuated her green eyes. But who was the man sitting next to Rita? He wore glasses and had a great suntan, surely Rita didn't have a boyfriend at her age, but she did seem to be very fond of him. He didn't seem to know many people here apart from Rita's family.

The crowded room had quietened down now that everyone was seated. Once the chimed glass had rung out Rita got up out of her seat and spoke to the assembled party. She sparkled more brightly than the Van Royen diamonds she wore.

'I want to thank you all for coming as my guests tonight. It means lot to me, especially those of you who have travelled from far away.'

She turned and her eyes rested on that man sitting next to her. There was a twinkle in her eye as she looked at the mysterious stranger. People, especially Faye, wondered if she had had a bit too much champagne. She seemed really very excited. She went on to thank everyone who had contributed and for coming to the launch of her charity. She spoke of the work she was hoping would be carried out both structural and physical work, the trust had bought the derelict *Castle Hotel* and planning permission had been applied for to convert it to a cultural centre. Rita had managed to cut swiftly through red tape, time was important to her, and her money talked. But as well as the hotel importance was also given to community work for the benefit of the people of the town she loved.

She reminisced about the old days when she first arrived in the town, how supportive everyone had been to her family and the other evacuees, and the change she had seen, then finally went on to introduce the guest of honour, '*Who had travelled from Australia to be with us.*' William Gerard, her younger brother (now seventy nine, but didn't look it!). She had been so overjoyed to be back in touch with one brother, and now she had two! She explained how he had come on the scene, then he stood and said a few words himself, about how he was looking forward to working with the charity and how he came to be there that night.

However had she found him? She put it down to '*cosmic ordering*' her thoughts had gone out to him. One day in the previous, August at home in Australia, while reminiscing about his early life, having tried to investigate his genealogy online for the first time, he decided to browse on the internet and had seen the editorial on the website of a local Welsh paper. He had googled the town he thought he had briefly been taken to when he was very young (they were very early memories, he was not absolutely sure about this), and he read about the controversy around the people of the town wanting to save the pier. He read of the launch of the new charity, Rita's story of her background, and after a little family research realised that she and Jimmy were his long lost sister and brother. He had been orphaned during the bombing of the Second World War in Liverpool, then put into a children's home. Emigrating as a twenty one year old '£10 pom' on the 'SS New Australia' in 1956. He was among the estimated 710,000 Britons seeking a new life in Australia who took advantage of the offer.

After a chequered career he had found work in the manufacture of Bricks and Tiles in South Australia, invested in them and never looked back (and he didn't say so but he was nearly as wealthy as Rita, perhaps wealthier.) He was recently widowed, and without children and along with Rita also wanted to contribute to the good of the town. Both he and Rita believed in the adage *'Of those to who much is given, much is expected.'*

Of course he had been given nothing, except perhaps an opportunity, and was a self-made man. Overwhelmed to be reunited with siblings he had thought lost for ever, he was eager for Rita to spend time with him in Australia during the winter months. He didn't think he would like the climate in Wales in the Winter, and he didn't want to lose touch with his friends in Oz. If Rita could afford the time away from her charity they would travel by ship, luxury liner.

2038 From the Noughties to the Forties

Colwyn Bay

Alexis Vetriano swung her long slim suntanned legs out of the car and stepped out from the back seat of the black and cream electric Armstrong Siddely and as she elevated herself on to killer patent leather high heels she looked around to see that other cars parked nearby were of equal calibre to hers. Nearby was an electric Rolls Royce limousine and a little further away a hydrogen powered Aston Martin sports car. She reached for her Italian designer briefcase containing not papers, but her I pads and 3d computer, then shook her tailored linen jacket before slipping it on. A floral fresh fragrance of lilies and roses hung in the air as she released her long dark silky hair loose from her collar, and as it swung down her back, green jewels caught the light glittering at her ears as she leaned towards the rolled down tinted window to speak to her chauffeuse about arrangements she had made to meet up with her later.

Alexis had a business meeting at the new conference centre but first she wanted to reacquaint herself with Colwyn Bay town. It had been some years since she had visited and she had family connections, many memories and legends, about which she wanted to reminisce and draw inspiration. She also wanted to see the difference, whether a decade's improvements here matched or exceeded those in other parts of the country. She would need to know a lot more details if her project was to go ahead and she was relying on this meeting today to get her up to speed.

As an arts graduate, responsible for events, her role was in planning and forecasting. One of the many centenary celebrations of this town would be the highlighting of the wartime contribution by the residents of the 1940s. Celebrations were to begin in a year's time, but needed much fine tuning. Her meeting was with a local councillor who had lived in the town for the past 30 years. She lifted her hand to her brow shielding her eyes from the sun, and looked around approvingly, getting re-acquainted with her previously familiar surroundings. This town had certainly benefited greatly from the regeneration programme of the last twenty years in an outstanding way. It had first started slowly in the late noughties just before she was born, and heaven knows it had needed it then. Other parts of the country also in desperate need of refurbishment had led the way so that this town followed, reinventing itself and it had benefited from the experiences and advice of the others. Alexis' grandmother Faye, to whom she was very close had been born here in the 1950s, and so had her grandfather who had tragically died in 1994. Although Grandma Faye had not lived here all her life she had returned to retire here and became intensely involved in restoration projects. Faye had brought Alexis' father Alex here often when he was a child to visit his grandparents back in the twentieth century and was thrilled that her young granddaughter responded to her, always wanting to know more, much more than Faye's son Alex ever had as a child. Alexis had grown up mesmerised by stories of her family background and heritage, this town where she had been at boarding school herself featuring largely in them and it was influences such as these that led her to study history and sociology. Yes, Alexis was fond of this place and pleased that her work had brought her here. It was always a pleasure to return and especially these days. Heritage work was a thriving industry, people valuing what they might otherwise lose. Tourism within the country had really taken off after the oil crises and carbon footprints, then there were the ash clouds of the second decade, which had deterred people from travelling abroad. The first of these had been in 2010 in Iceland and many more had followed. That, along with the threat of terrorism in those days made it unsafe to travel. Therefore 'staycations' had become ever more popular and boosted the economy in this and other coastal towns.

She wandered, fascinated, among the beautifully restored buildings. The work had been meticulously completed, paying attention to authentic details with highly skilled and trained artists and craftsmen using the best quality materials and newest innovative techniques. Apart from the vehicles and the dress of the passers-by she would have thought she was back in Victorian times or the set of a film of those days. Standards were as high as she had seen in the superb recreations in the historic town of Williamsburg in the United States and nearer home at Port Sunlight.

She stopped outside an imposing former hotel building called. 'The Metropole'. She had heard the name before and was struggling to remember in what context. Strangely she really felt some affinity with this building, that she had been here before, or would return here. She flicked back her hair with her hand and leaned down and spoke into the gold 'watchphone', on her lapel, using it as a dictaphone to record her impressions and made notes to which she would return to research it. Suddenly she looked around, she had distinctly felt someone watching her, but no, whoever it was had gone. How odd, she shivered with apprehension. Her attention then focussed on the horse drawn carriages waiting outside with liveried drivers, awaiting participants who were attending events inside. They were certainly watching curiously this young woman with star quality. She walked up the steps under a jewel- like stained glass canopy and entered by gently pushing back the swing doors, heavily ornamented with highly polished brass plates. To the left of the reception there was a ballroom, with a polished wooden floor and wall to wall mirrors where a class of children wearing pastel coloured tutus were practising ballet. She felt she was travelling back in time, at least a century ago, since she had heard of a description of this hotel as it was in the twentieth century. Back in the early part of the C21st the entire ground floor of this building had been reclaimed from flats. Turning she looked beyond the reception to an elegant restaurant where original oil paintings with heavy carved gold frames, beautifully lit, adorned the dark evergreen walls. Guests seemed to be deep in absorbing conversations while the stimulating aroma of coffee permeated the air. Gleaming silver coffee pots adorned the snow-white tablecloths; waiters and waitresses in black with immaculate starched white aprons were in attendance. Clients were not only partaking of coffee in conventional cups, but giant glass globes were evident on each table, in which small quantities of essence were placed and '*diners*' were inhaling through straws; essence of lemon pie or tomato soup were being experienced as the new aerosol cuisines, breathable foods. This had been developed by an American in the noughties, but grew in popularity in Paris the gastronomic capital and spread throughout the world. Those diners who were eating more traditional food were employing '*technoplates*', whereby each morsel added to the plate was analysed by use of '*tags*' which relayed messages to their '*watchphones*', about content, additives, calorific allowance for the day. This facility had its infancy at around the time of Alexis' childhood but was commonplace now and widely employed, a boon to those with dietary requirements and an aid to good health.

Retro, but with a timeless quality, C20th jazz played in the background. Alexis appreciated the sophisticated ambiance and thought to herself how lovely it would have been, if only she had realised its existence, to have arranged her meeting here. Maybe next time, she went on her way thinking of the future possibilities of venues since she fully intended to return, it would be necessary to finalise arrangements for the project.

On leaving she took out of her leather case a small vial about the size of a lipstick, her *whif* (a miniature version of the *whaf* bowls seen in the restaurant) and inhaled some powdered chocolate to give herself an energy boost. Thus fortified, continuing down the street she noticed a number of clothes shops displaying high fashion on the mannequins, while shoppers and business people passing by appeared very well turned out, immaculate in fact, taking great pride in their appearance. Not necessarily expensively dressed, but well-coordinated, as if they had put thought into what they would wear, and their peace of mind which enabled them to do this was evident. The era of throwaway disposable clothing was for ecological reasons now history, and accordingly the sweatshop import trade was long gone. There were well dressed people of *all* age groups present, although this was still largely a retirement community, of course the retirement age was higher than it had ever been, and life expectancy had also risen. The pensioners she had seen passing by, browsing, window shopping, chatting happily and laughing seemed a lively bunch. She put this down to the alleged high quality of living perhaps. Back in the old days in about 2020 when she had visited as a child she remembered that the town had still seemed full of people with little prospect of work, living without hope in houses of multiple occupation paid for by what used to be called ' *benefits*.' She had also heard it had been called '*Well Fare*'. The drugs problems of this and other towns had by 2038 been largely eradicated. Gone were the days of austerity and poverty which lingered on from 2010 with the first of the Coalition governments and the following years, the days of her childhood. How life had changed for the better for everyone since peace was eventually achieved after the dreadful and tragic wars in the Middle East.

Alexis had done some research with her Grandma Faye's input, but wanted to know so much more. She wanted to promote a centenary event here to mark the anniversary of the Second World War. She would have so loved to talk to the people who had lived in the town during wartime, but it had ended in 1945 some years before her eighty eight year old Grandma was born. Faye was fortunate enough to have liaised with them. The stories had become even more fascinating now that they were no longer accessible, that was always the way.

'*Meeting due to start in fifteen minutes.*' Her combination '*watch phone*' announced to her from a magnetic lapel pin, popularised by the Queen. Wristwatches had gone out of style in the twenty twenties when she was a child, since people then used their phones to tell the time. But they had morphed into the style of old watches on gold chains with all the benefits and advantages state of the art technology could provide within them including magnets to balance the body. Expertise had advanced in leaps and bounds in the mid-21st century and Britain was a leader in technological advances once again, boosting the economy dramatically. But sociologically some of the older regimes and principles were being retrospectively appreciated and reinstated. For example, crime had decreased dramatically following a return to solid family values and standards. Lessons had been learned from the past, and moralities had grown stronger with the royal family, William, Catherine and their son George Prince of Wales and siblings, one of whom looked very like her late grandmother.

Alexis made her way past the station, which she was surprised to see still here, in the days of super-electric motors and helibuses, but it was restored now to its original state of Victoriana. This was not the original site of the first railway, no she remembered what she had learned, there had first been the 'Pwllychrochan Halt', built for the Erskine family who had first settled in that wonderful mansion near the woods. She remembered the main station, central to the town as it had been when she was a child, and the stories she had heard about all the evacuee children arriving from Liverpool in the Second World War. This new station building was a refurbishment in character, taste and function. But while basing plans on old styles, new methods and materials improved the results. Rail travel was faster these days and kept as a pleasurable activity for outings. The route had been diverted so that traffic of electric non- polluting cars flowed freely from the town to the seafront as it used to do when first built and the petrol driven cars had gone down that road. There was also a footbridge across the A55 at which she crossed the road on to the promenade. '*What an improvement*' thought Alexis, 'on *the way it was when I was a girl*'. First she took in the sight of the vast expanse of clean golden sands and the sweep of the bay drinking in the clean sea air and thinking, '*some things never change*', then she looked over at the Pier entrance in amazement. The outer entrance was a Victorian replica of the original, but as she passed through towards the main building she found it was the perfect blend of traditional and state of the art modernity. Steel, wood, and glass, an engraved crystal town emblem of oak leaves shone proudly. King William will approve of this, she thought to herself. (The King and Queen were very fond of North Wales, since King William had trained and worked in Anglesey as a helicopter pilot, during their courtship and the couple spent the early years of their marriage there.) The King, as his father had been, was an aficionado of great architecture. There was a plaque to say that Queen Catherine had opened the new conference centre, near the health and fitness hub on the pier in 2030. That of course was the second wave of regeneration, the first in the year Alexis was born in the Elizabethan era, was when the pier had been restored and saved from demolition, as the people insisted passionately through public outcry. It had caused the biggest stir for many years, with packed meetings in the old St Paul's church and hall in the centre of town, Grandma Faye had attended. But since the improvement in the British economy in the following decade and the diligence of those agitating for funding there was money to design and build the conference centre of wood, steel and glass with domes and spires, reminiscent of the very first pavilion built. Technological advances had made it possible. The whole seafront was vastly improved of course; especially since the eyesores of wind farms had been more discretely placed, (and would ultimately be replaced with improved methods.) They had never been popular with the people who had never been asked or consulted before they were installed, but they had achieved an income to aid the regeneration schemes. In 2038 global warming was no longer an issue and neither was the planet dependent on fossil fuels, an issue resolved through miraculously improved technology.

Alexis entered across the barrier by using the usual method of iris recognition, which had been employed for some decades. Her vivid green eyes fringed with dark lashes disclosed her entire profile to the monitor and activated the message. '*Welcome Ms Vetriano*' the automated but invisible ' *barrier*' announced in English and in Welsh ' *You are expected in suite' Pedwar' please make your way to the first floor'*. The system had been programmed to expect her and had instantly vetted her through access to her personal history. Advanced technology was another reason why crime had subsided, providing greater security and methods of detection. She made her way to the glass lift and to the suite '*Pedwar*'in the pier's conference centre where her contact waited. She was glad to know that the Welsh language was alive and used more than ever in the mid C21st .

A distinguished looking man, tall and slim, with grey wavy hair and who appeared to be in his fifties, stood up to greet her as he saw her approach. He was immaculately suited and well groomed. 'Mr Johnson? ' she questioned ' Yes, *Good morning Ms Vetriano*' He said warmly, '*we spoke on the phone, I have been so looking forward to meeting you,*' she replied, '*Please call me Alexis*' they had instant rapport. '*Sure, Alexis and do call me Liam.*'

* * *

Liam and Alexis were still talking animatedly some time later. Liam was telling Alexis everything she wanted to know.

'*And so the museum and new learning centre was built in the converted church just across the road from the library which had been left derelict for years and years, what a shocking state that was in. There were plans to convert it into flats but the building didn't really lend itself to a design for living space,*' said Liam. '*Or so I was told by my Grandad, and he was an architect.*'

'Yes,' agreed Alexis. '*It wouldn't have appealed to retirees anyway.*'

Liam continued. '*We had needed a museum for some time, I*

mean how can you collect and preserve things when there is nowhere to put them for people to appreciate them. A lot of valuable items had already gone into skips over the years. And it's not just objects which were lost, but experiences. Now there are oral histories stored there from people who lived through the Second World War, they were collected.... starting in 2010 and first stored in the library, and it's still an on-going project, they are collecting from the year 2014 onwards now. Of course these days it is so much easier to track peoples life paths through technology, 'big brother' is very active everywhere, with newer technologies, but had they not collected those stories in the noughties then valuable information would have been lost, locked away in human memory.'

'Yes, I agree', Alexis enthused. *'Faye my Grandma was actively involved in the early years of that project; in fact she told me it was she who proposed it'.*

'Well we are so glad she did,' said Liam, *'or so much would have been lost. We still have not yet had that breakthrough we expect with time travel, but I am convinced we are on the brink of it. When I was a boy people used to laugh at such ideas, but now they are not so sceptical.'*

Alexis nodded in agreement. *' Sure, I will be signing up for it as soon as possible, in fact...'* She wondered for a moment, should she really confide such a disclosure to a man she had just met? But went ahead anyway. *'I have had an extraordinary episode of 'déjà vu' today, on Penrhyn Road, it was outside the Metropole....'* Alexis was dreaming of such a time when she could travel to the past, and had promised herself that when her chance came her first trial would be in this town, and probably at The Metropole building.

'Anyway,' said Liam, not prepared to go down that route, *'I would think the collected archives of the noughties will be an important source of information to you.'*

'Absolutely, you are so right,' agreed Alexis. 'I can't wait to hear them, and read the transcriptions, and you know I have so enjoyed meeting you and hearing news about this town.'

'Yes this has been a very good meeting,' said Liam. 'Pleasurable as well as extremely useful and thought provoking. I am certain your plans will produce an excellent event, with the right support. I like your ideas, we will meet again soon to discuss this further when I have reported back to my colleagues, and if there is anything at all we can help you with do ask. But now, tell me more about your connections to this town, and... how is it that you have an Italian name?'

Alexis laughed and shook back her mane of silky hair, her green peridot earrings glittered. 'I married an Italian who I met on business in Verona. But in the old days my parents used to bring me here for holidays as a young child. I liked it here so much that when they suggested I should be at boarding school while they travelled with my father's work I jumped at the chance to be near my grandmother. And I have other family near here, a cousin in Llandudno who has an hotel. His name is Ethan and he is almost the same age as me. My grandmother Faye lives not far from here and I am very close to her. She is eighty eight now, but she still gets around and is very active. She visits me in London often. It's to her that I owe my passion for history and recreating events like this. I hope I will be as dynamic as she is when I am her age. I think a lot of older people here enjoy good health... there is something in the air... and what about you? Have your family always lived here?'

Liam looked thoughtful. 'My grandfather was evacuated here in the Second World War from Liverpool, with his brother and sister, they were from a very poor family. Then when we were children he used to bring us here for holidays in the 1990s. The town was in decline then in those days but we enjoyed coming here, and hearing his childhood memories of wartime. I moved here myself when I was in my twenties and met Grace, my wife here. She was a nurse then, I met her through her work. Well actually I was her patient.'

Alexis looked concerned and was about to ask if he had served in the forces, when Liam saw her expression. '*Don't ask. We won't go into that, it's another story, anyway, Grace's family are nearby so we settled here... But going back to the wartime days, and my grandfather – his younger brother was taken back to Liverpool before the end of the war by their mother, you see the bombing hadn't properly started then... then when it did... he... that is Billy... and his Mum who was my great grandmother disappeared... and...Jimmy... my grandfather and his sister thought they were dead. I was named after him... Uncle William I mean. He had been rescued from a bombsite but they couldn't identify him and he had apparently lost his speech for some time through trauma and needed medical attention. He had been living in an orphanage then he turned up alive years later in Australia of all places, and had made a great success of his life after going out as one of the £10 immigrants in the 1950s. He was able to trace us through news of this town on the internet. It was at that time when the townspeople were making waves about saving the pier from demolition. Of course we didn't even realise he was still alive!*'

'*Really?*' said Alexis, fascinated. She had always loved a good story. '*That's wonderful, that you found each other, and that he was so successful.*'

'*Yes, in construction,*' said Liam. '*Brick and tile manufacture. So he was well placed to give my Great Aunt Rita advice on her building projects, as that was his business.*'

Alexis went on. '*But sad that you lost him for so many years. And what about the sister?*'

Liam paused before asking, '*Did you ever hear of Margarita Gerard the singer?*'

'*Oh yes of course*', said Alexis, her eyes were shining. '*Oh, that Rita! My Grandma Faye used to work for her, as a kind of personal assistant or companion. Look these green ear-rings I am wearing, they were once hers and she gave them to grandma Faye. It was while she was living in Spain about thirty years ago, a few years before I was born. Then she came back to live here, she kept in touch with Grandma Faye, but didn't need her as much, not after Rita started the Foundation' and Grandma was busy and into projects herself. But they were very close at one time and I know she was really sad when Rita died.'*

'Yes,' said Liam, *'we all were. I know she was very elderly and had had a good life, but that cure for cancer was a long time coming. These days people have a much better chance of survival, almost a hundred percent. And we were so touched that she left a huge amount of money to the regeneration fund, and the Foundation. We had no idea how wealthy she was... My wife's grandmother, Muriel knew her back in the old days too before she became famous.'*

'No neither did Faye know of the extent of her wealth, she kept that quiet,' said Alexis, *'she was so unassuming. I don't really know much about Rita's background and her early life. I mean we knew she had a good career herself, but wasn't her late husband one of the Belgian refugee diamantieres who worked on tools for navigation instruments produced on the North Wales coast during the Second World War?'*

'Yes,' said Liam, *'he was from one of those families. He remained in the diamond business when he returned to Belgium after the war, then they met there during one of her tours as a singer. He had seen her dance on stage when they were children, they had a shared background in this town. But her legacy to the town really started the ball rolling. You see all those people who wanted this pier saved... they had to contribute.'*

'Yes I see,' Alexis continued. *'Without first the support of various funding , then also your Great Aunt Rita's input... there just wouldn't have been enough money for it. Grandma always said that those years*

208

of austerity were a turning point, and that people started to become less materialistic, more altruistic, less self-centred. People stopped striving for unattainable goals, for fame at all cost without talent and the cult of vacuous celebrity started to wane.'

Liam was still talking about Rita, who had been very talented, but had appreciated the encouragement she had been given. *'She loved this town and was so grateful for her shelter here during the War, and the people who helped her start her career. Of course she was a natural performer, she started her days in entertainment on the pier stage and various hotel ballrooms. 'The Castle' was the one I always remember, I was taken there for holidays as a child. Being there and hearing stories about the old days certainly influenced me. You know she converted that hotel into a cultural centre in 2016 when it had become derelict. I remember the beautiful scenic murals painted on the walls. When they renovated it they were found, they had been safely boxed in.'*

Alexis remembered some of what her Grandma had told her. *'But her career wouldn't have taken off without the help she got from the wartime community in this town?'*

'Yes. She was indebted and people like to repay kindnesses.' Liam sighed. *'Certainly, this town contributed a lot, not only to the evacuees, but in all sorts of other ways that were never acknowledged until later. I was sad to see how the town had deteriorated when I returned here in the late noughties.'* Then he brightened, saying, *'But look at it now, isn't it miraculous?'*

Through the connections they had both Alexis and Liam began to think that they were practically related, and that fate had brought them together. But by the laws of the *six stages of separation* they were bound to have some sort of a connection in a small town like this. So many others had, and it gave them a sense of community, which helped them work together to the same purpose for the good of the town, in which they delighted.

This applied not only those who had always lived there, but also those who returned, because they felt their roots were there.

'Yes, you are so right,' said Alexis. 'What goes around comes around. Can we look at the holograms in the information showcases, and those plaques on our way out? I think some of them have been here for almost thirty years. Let's see who else we both knew.'

* * *

Faye sat alone on her rocking chair gazing at the view out of her window, a black and white cat circled her feet and she got up to make her way to the kitchen to fetch a saucer of milk. Faye was eighty eight now, but she felt she was more like sixty eight, and very fit. She had many memories, which she constantly revived and relived. Some had been recorded by school students from the Heritage project and stored in the archive.

Not content with revisiting the past she aimed to make new memories and was planning another trip to London to visit her son and daughter-in-law, who were soon to be grandparents. Alexis, she had just heard, was pregnant. 'Ha,' thought Faye, 'That wouldn't stop her working on the event she planned for the following year,' it was well under way now. Faye herself still had projects in mind and was looking forward to meeting up with her friend Ella to discuss them. She always looked to the future.